It was definitely her.

When she'd settled inside and the limo pulled out onto the street, Dakota followed. A few turns and twenty-one minutes later, the car stopped in front of a run-down building on a deserted street.

When Lucky Malone climbed out of the car, Dakota's attention zeroed in on her. She had a killer body. Even the conservative dress pants couldn't hide a backside like that. The equally modest blouse tightened over nicely rounded breasts as she moved. She said something to the driver before closing the door, then seemed to brace herself before entering the building.

Dakota slid out of his truck and hustled to the other end of the alley. It was quiet, until a low roar put him on alert. The roar grew louder until a dark sedan skidded to a stop between him and Malone's limo.

The sedan's front doors flew open. Two men bailed out and rushed Malone's car. Dakota heard two unmistakable sounds. Silenced gunshots.

A new kind of tension ignited in Dakota's veins.

A hit team. The driver was dead…and Malone would be next.

DEBRA WEBB

DAMAGED

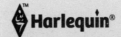
Harlequin®

TORONTO NEW YORK LONDON
AMSTERDAM PARIS SYDNEY HAMBURG
STOCKHOLM ATHENS TOKYO MILAN MADRID
PRAGUE WARSAW BUDAPEST AUCKLAND

This book is dedicated to the sweetest little boy, Dakota Bailey, and his awesome mom, Lynn Bailey. I'm so glad you're family.

Recycling programs for this product may not exist in your area.

ISBN-13: 978-0-373-69544-7

DAMAGED

Copyright © 2011 by Debra Webb

www.eHarlequin.com

Printed in U.S.A.

ABOUT THE AUTHOR

Debra Webb wrote her first story at age nine and her first romance at thirteen. It wasn't until she spent three years working for the military behind the Iron Curtain and within the confining political walls of Berlin, Germany, that she realized her true calling. A five-year stint with NASA on the space shuttle program reinforced her love of the endless possibilities within her grasp as a storyteller. A collision course between suspense and romance was set. Debra has been writing romantic suspense and action-packed romantic thrillers since. Visit her at www.DebraWebb.com or write to her at P.O. Box 4889, Huntsville, AL 35815.

Books by Debra Webb

CAST OF CHARACTERS

Dakota Garrett—Former military, Garrett is a member of the new Equalizers. His only concern is getting the job done.

Lucky Malone—Brand-new at the Colby Agency, a quick errand for Lucas Camp combined with a secret she must keep for Victoria Colby-Camp draws Lucky into a race for her own life as well as Victoria's.

Dr. Lionel Byrd—He has turned the secretive Byrd Institute into a place that inspires fear. Only one person has ever escaped his special method of treatment. Byrd will do anything to ensure Dakota Garrett doesn't escape again.

Victoria Colby-Camp—Victoria is facing possibly the biggest challenge of her life. Can she protect those she loves or will fate prove a foe she cannot defeat?

Lucas Camp—He is certain the new owner of the Equalizers is up to something dangerous…something that involves the Colby Agency. Can he find the truth in time to protect those he loves?

Jim Colby—When he sold the Equalizers to an unnamed buyer, he had his doubts. Has he made a mistake he will live to regret?

Ian Michaels and Simon Ruhl—The Colby Agency's seconds-in-command.

Mildred Ballard—Victoria's personal assistant. She never misses a day at the agency and Victoria has no secrets from Mildred. Mildred never imagined that a rare day at the spa would take her from the office at a time when the schemes of two men would coalesce into a dangerous game where Victoria's life is the prize.

Chapter One

Dakota Garrett waited in the darkness.

The garage smelled faintly of gasoline and oil. The mark evidently preferred servicing his vehicles at home. He didn't look the type in his meticulously pressed suits and little bow ties. How many high-level accountants could, much less would, change the oil in the family sedan? Only one terrified of trusting another with any aspect of the family vehicle's operation.

Darnell Raspberry manipulated and supervised every asset possessed by his boss, Devon Wallace—the single most powerful man in the Midwest. Wallace had built an empire of wealth and power during the latter half of his life. Too bad he'd started using innocent people as his stepping stones. One of those people had come to the Equalizers for help. Wallace operated above the law. And, thus far, no one had been able to stop him.

It wasn't Dakota's job to stop Wallace. He could care less about the man or his activities. At some point in the past half decade he'd stopped analyzing right from wrong. Dakota's singular goal was to accomplish his mission.

Get the job done.

What else was there?

For him…nothing.

Anger whispered through him, making his jaw clench. Dakota pushed it away. The past was the past. Dead and gone. Emphasis on the dead. He operated in the moment and only in the moment.

Justice could be served outside a courtroom. That was sufficient for Dakota's conscience.

The door leading from the kitchen of the Raspberry home to the dark garage opened. Dakota braced for action.

Darnell Raspberry stepped into the garage and carefully locked the door behind him. The three quiet tones that followed assured him that he'd properly set the home's elaborate security system.

The makers obviously hadn't counted on someone like Dakota Garrett needing to get past their so-called state-of-the-art system. For him, cutting off the link to the home's attached garage had been as effortless as taking his next breath. Raspberry had no clue that a cold, harsh reality waited for him just a few steps away.

Raspberry rounded the hood of his two-door hybrid, the one he used for traveling to and from work. Nothing pricey, not at all like the fine home attached to the double-car garage or the luxury sedan he'd purchased for his family. The garage's overhead light as well as the interior one in the vehicle stayed dark as Raspberry climbed into the driver's seat. The smart little accountant had thought of everything. He had a careful routine. Don't turn on the light. Start the engine and hit the remote. Barrel out of the garage and close the door.

His goal was simple: protect his nice little family.

Didn't matter that his boss ruined the lives of nice little families every day.

The hybrid's engine started. Dakota pushed away from the wall. Until the vehicle shifted out of Park, both doors would remain unlocked. Dakota had the passenger-side door open before the unsuspecting man had time to blink or to shift into Reverse.

Dakota pressed the muzzle of his weapon to Raspberry's pale temple. "Drive to the office as usual," he ordered, "and we won't have a problem."

Raspberry's eyes bulged with fear. The faint lighting from the dash allowed him a peek at Dakota from the corners of his eyes. "What do you want?"

Dakota breathed a chuckle. "To make an honest man out of you, Darnell."

"I…" Raspberry swallowed hard. "I don't understand."

"Just drive." Dakota applied a bit more pressure.

"No."

The protest surprised Dakota. He hadn't figured the man for the gutsy type. "Fine. We'll just do this right here."

A gasp imprisoned the accountant's breath. "But... but my family..."

"Still asleep in their beds." Dakota knew precisely where each member of the Raspberry family was at the moment. East and west ends of the second floor. The master suite was actually on the first, but the wife didn't like being so far away from the kiddies. She and the two kids didn't rise until seven.

"What do you want?" Raspberry asked again.

"To take care of business without having to bother with the nasty business of killing anyone."

"My family has nothing to do with my work," the accountant argued, his confidence seeming to build since Dakota hadn't put a bullet in his brain just yet. "They're completely innocent."

Impatience nudged Dakota. "True, but, as you well know, innocence matters little in the grand scheme of things. Now, let's go."

Raspberry's fingers tightened on the steering wheel. "What if I refuse?"

Well, well, more of that unexpected bravado. "Then I'll have to go in there and drum up a little motivation." Dakota grunted his regret. "I never did like to frighten small children." He leaned close to the man who was his mark. "But that doesn't mean I won't do my very best if necessary."

"All right. All right." Hand shaking, Raspberry tapped the garage door remote pinned to his sun visor and shifted the vehicle into Reverse.

"Very good, Darnell."

As soon as he'd backed into the drive, Raspberry hit the remote again, closing the garage door. Once in the street, he pointed the hybrid in the direction of the Wallace Building.

"You'll never get past security," Raspberry charged. "The Wallace Building has the best security available."

Dakota smiled. "I won't have to get past security. We'll enter the building from the parking garage, just like you do every morning. You arrive well before anyone else so it'll be just the two of us."

Raspberry shifted in his seat, fear and tension obviously making him uncomfortable. "What about the video surveillance? Security will see you in the garage."

Dakota lowered his weapon, but kept a bead on the rattled man. "Details, details. You don't need to concern yourself with those. All you have to do is exactly what I tell you."

The fact was Dakota had planned for that nuisance. Security would indeed capture him arriving in the parking garage with Raspberry. And when the two of them boarded the elevator, Dakota would scan an authorized entry badge. Security might not know the face or the name, but they wouldn't be able to deny the approved access. Questions would be asked later, but Dakota would be long gone by then.

"You'll never get away with this." Raspberry shook his head. "The police will have your description. Your face will be all over the news. You'll be a wanted man."

"Probably." Dakota wasn't the slightest bit worried. The face the security cameras would record was not one that could ever be connected to Dakota Garrett. His mother had never been a true mother to Dakota, but she had passed on to him an invaluable asset—the art of disguise.

A lifetime ago.

"Are you going to kill me?"

The bravado had vanished. If Raspberry's voice had been any smaller it would have been inaudible.

"Not unless I have to." No point lying to the man.

"What're you going to do?"

Dakota leaned in close to the driver again, making him shudder in fear. "I'm going to take back what your boss stole from his clients."

Raspberry seemed to chew on that for a moment. "One of Mr. Wallace's competitors sent you," he accused. "I should have known."

"Nope." Dakota relaxed into the seat. "I have no affiliations with any of his competitors."

"You're a thief." A nuance of anger shadowed the words.

"I've been called worse."

"Mr. Wallace will hunt you down and make you pay."

"He'll try."

"He'll kill me." Raspberry's voice quaked.

"Possibly." Even the best resources were at times tossed away. Wallace wouldn't hesitate to find himself another accountant. Finding one as talented as Mr. Raspberry might take some time though. "That's why," Dakota offered, "when we're done I would rush home, pack up my little family and disappear."

Raspberry shot him a look. "How am I supposed to do that? You can't give me witness protection."

Dakota shrugged. "True. But that nest egg you've been building all these years should take care of you and your family quite nicely for the rest of your lives. You're a man of above-average intelligence, I'm certain you'll find the perfect place to become invisible."

Raspberry had no rebuttal for Dakota's suggestions.

Downtown Chicago came into view. They were close now. Dakota checked his wristwatch. Right on time.

"This is insane. You'll never get away with this."

"I guess we'll know soon enough." The subject had grown boring.

"If he doesn't have you exterminated like a bug,"

Raspberry warned, "you'll spend the rest of your life in prison."

Dakota had to laugh at that one. "I don't think your boss is going to call the police."

"He…he…" Raspberry's face turned as red as the succulent fruit his forefathers had no doubt grown, earning the surname. "He has friends in high places in law enforcement."

"An official investigation is the last thing your boss would want," Dakota countered. "I'm certain you're aware of the extent to which he goes in order to cover his illegal activities." Raspberry was a master at fixing the books. Wallace had experts all around him, shielding his every move. He wouldn't like this one little bit, but unless he could resolve it without involving the police, he would take it like a loss in the stock market. This was the risk one took when gambling with the highest stakes.

"Who are you?" Raspberry braked at a light and dared to meet Dakota's eyes.

Dakota could tell him that he was an Equalizer and that he was here to equalize the situation, but he wouldn't. "I'm the man who's giving you a chance to do the right thing, Darnell."

"It's probably the last thing I'll do," he mumbled.

Possibly. That, too, was the chance a man took when he chose the dark side.

Dakota knew this from experience.

Problem was, once a man crossed that line, finding

his way back was not a straight or an easy path. The line was blurred, the way obscured.

And nothing ever looked the same through the haze that lingered after that waltz on the dark side.

Not even in the bright light of day.

Chapter Two

Lucky Malone stopped on the sidewalk and peered up at the gleaming building before her. Her pulse scrambled with the pounding in her chest.

She really worked here.

A smile spread across her lips.

The Colby Agency.

Her life was perfect now.

Absolutely perfect.

"You'll get over that soon enough."

Lucky turned to the man who'd spoken. Lucas Camp. *The* Lucas Camp. She recaptured the breath that had rushed from her lungs at the sound of his voice and her lips stretched back into that big smile without any prompting. "Good morning, Mr. Camp." Good grief, she must look like a total idiot standing out here staring up at the building this way.

His wise gray eyes glittered with mirth but his lips never even twitched. "Good morning, Ms. Malone."

He gave her a quick once-over and nodded in approval. "You look fully prepared to launch into your second week on the job with Victoria."

"I'm looking forward to the challenge, sir."

For one long moment he studied her, as if assessing the comment.

Fear banded around her chest. "I mean the opportunity. I'm looking forward to the opportunity."

This time Mr. Camp smiled. "I know what you mean." He touched a hand to her elbow. "Come along and let's see if Mildred has a pot of her famous coffee brewed already. Maybe Simon or Ian showed up with donuts."

"That would be nice." Lucky had to work extra hard to keep those donuts and pastries she loved from showing on her hips. There was nothing in the world like a warm, gooey, sweet donut with coffee.

She entered the lobby with Mr. Camp. Flashing a smile for security as she passed, she boarded the waiting elevator car. Mr. Camp stepped in right behind her and selected the fourth floor, then propped against the wall as the car bumped into motion.

A knot of fear abruptly twisted in Lucky's stomach.

She would never, not in a bazillion years, be able to make a pot of coffee the way Mildred did. Lucky bit her lip. Maybe she could buy the coffee across the street at Maggie's Coffee House and then pretend she'd made it.

Mildred Ballard, Victoria's personal assistant,

single-handedly kept the office running smoothly. She knew the assignments of every investigator on staff. Not to mention their birthdays, anniversaries and kids' names. She worked magic with travel arrangements. And her coffee was famous.

Lucky would never be that good at any of those things.

Anxiety inched its way up her spine.

She wanted to keep this job.

If she proved good enough, maybe one day she would be a Colby agent. That was her ultimate goal. Meanwhile, she was starting out as Mildred's backup.

The elevator doors slid open to an empty lobby on the fourth floor. Other than the top echelon of investigators, most of the staff didn't arrive until seven-thirty—unless there was a special meeting.

As Lucky walked side by side with Lucas Camp along the main corridor, the realization that he had arrived at the office without Victoria took primacy above all the other thoughts whirling around in Lucky's head.

"Mrs. Colby-Camp isn't coming into the office today?" Lucky wouldn't have to be so worried about making a mistake while shadowing Mildred if that were the case.

"She's having breakfast with a friend this morning," Mr. Camp said as he held open the staff lounge door. The fragrant smell of coffee greeted them.

Lucky nodded. "Oh."

Being the consummate gentleman, Mr. Camp poured Lucky then himself a cup of Mildred's amazing coffee. "You know, Lucky," he said, his expression thoughtful, "I could use a small favor this morning." He picked up his cup of coffee, sipped it and hummed his approval.

Anticipation zinged Lucky. "Absolutely, sir. Anything you need." *Slow down, Lucky. Don't act like a fan-girl.* She cleared her throat. "I'm happy to be of service." *Better.*

"Let's go to my office."

Lucas Camp's office sat directly across the hall from Victoria's intimate waiting room. Mildred had told Lucky that the office Lucas now used had been an additional supply room, but one would never know it. Sophisticated was the first word to come to mind as Lucky entered the spacious office. A massive mahogany desk dominated the space. One wall was lined with distinguished-looking books, while another showcased numerous accolades, some of which were signed by the president himself. Like Victoria's office, his desk sat before an enormous window with an inspiring view. Two upholstered chairs waited in grand style before his desk.

Mr. Camp unlocked his desk and retrieved a small package. About the size of a jeweler's box, one made for a necklace or bracelet, the package was wrapped in brown paper. He passed it across his desk. Lucky shifted her coffee to her left hand and accepted the package.

She smiled. "A special occasion coming up?"

"You could say that," he answered without the slightest hint of discernible sentiment in his voice.

Lucky didn't make too much of his noncommittal tone or his unreadable expression. A man like Lucas Camp didn't give away what was on his mind unless he wanted to. A lifetime of working under deep cover with the CIA had made him an expert in covert operations and interrogations and a lot of other stuff Lucky couldn't begin to name, much less understand.

"I'd like you to take the package to an old friend of mine," he explained.

Lucky's pulse started that erratic race again. "An old friend?"

He scribbled something onto a notepad then tore off the page. "Here's the address. My friend is expecting the package this morning."

"I understand, sir." She glanced at the address. It was not one she recognized.

"I'm sure the area is unfamiliar to you so take a taxi," Mr. Camp suggested. "Have the driver wait. You'll only be a moment."

"Do I need a receipt as proof of delivery?" She wanted to do this right. Keeping Lucas Camp happy would be an important step up the ladder at the agency.

"There will be a verbal message," Mr. Camp explained. "The message is the only receipt I need."

"Yes, sir." Lucky turned to go but then hesitated.

"Your friend's name is…?" She certainly didn't want to make the mistake of leaving the package with the wrong person. Honestly, she didn't want to make any kind of mistake at all.

"Jennifer."

"Okay." Lucky had just assumed the friend was another man. Good thing she asked. "I'll be on my way, then."

"Report back to me as soon as you've made the drop," Mr. Camp said as she exited his office.

Lucky nodded. "Yes, sir."

She crossed the hall to inform Mildred that she had an errand, but Victoria's waiting room was empty, as was her office.

Lucky headed for the lounge to see if Mildred might be whipping up another pot of her amazing coffee. No Mildred in the lounge. Confused, she turned back toward Mildred's office.

"Lucky, there you are."

She kicked aside her confusion and posted a smile for Simon Ruhl, one of the agency's top investigators. He and Ian Michaels served as seconds-in-command to Victoria and her son, Jim. "Good morning, Mr. Ruhl." Wow, she was popular this morning.

Simon offered his usual friendly smile. "I just wanted to let you know that Mildred won't be back in the office until later this afternoon. She dropped by to make coffee, but then rushed away more giddy than I've seen her in ages." He smiled. "She's having a makeover, compliments of Victoria."

"Nice." Lucky hoped that wasn't something she was supposed to know already. Mildred hadn't mentioned the appointment. "Is it Mildred's birthday?"

Simon shook his head. "Her wedding anniversary is this week. Victoria wanted her to take the whole day off but Mildred insisted on stopping by and tying up any loose ends before leaving on her long weekend."

Tying up loose ends was just another way of saying she wanted to make sure Lucky was prepared for her short absence.

"That's really nice," she said to Mr. Ruhl. All the more reason she felt immensely fortunate for having landed this position. The Colby Agency was like one big family. "I have an errand to run for Mr. Camp. Will my being out for an hour or so be a problem?" Victoria might not like having her assistant and her new assistant-in-training out of the office at the same time. The point of having a backup was to ensure Victoria always had an assistant on duty.

"We've got it covered," Mr. Ruhl assured her. "Take care of Lucas's errand. Let me know when you're back in the office."

"Yes, sir."

Lucky started for the elevator again.

"One more thing, Lucky."

She turned back to him once more. "Sir?"

He gifted her with another of those warm smiles. "The sir isn't necessary. Nor is the mister. We're very informal around here. Call me Simon."

She nodded. That would take some getting used to. Where she was from, one always addressed their superiors and seniors in such a way.

Simon Ruhl chuckled as he walked away.

Lucky relaxed a little. She would be okay. Everyone seemed to like her so far. Then reality dropped down on her like a rock slide. She wouldn't have Mildred to keep her straight when Victoria arrived. A lump settled in Lucky's stomach.

Don't borrow trouble, she told herself. She would be fine. Her boss would surely understand the need for guidance with someone so new.

This time she actually reached her destination without being waylaid. She pressed the elevator's call button and took a couple of deep breaths in an effort to relax. They didn't really help.

In the lobby she waved at the two security guards as she strode toward the front entrance. The weather was beautiful. If she knew her way around a little better she would walk to the drop point. But getting lost was not a risk she wanted to take. And she wasn't actually sure of the distance.

She'd no more passed through the towering plate-glass doors when a big black car with the darkly tinted windows of a limo pulled to a stop in front of her. The parking area at the front of the building was rather small, mostly for short-term parking and drop-offs. Lucky made a sharp left to go around the car.

The rear window powered down. Lucky hesitated.

Maybe someone needed directions. She, unfortunately, wasn't the person to ask. Three months in the
city and she still got lost all too frequently. Chicago
was very different from Houston in climate and in
the way the city was laid out.

"Good morning, Lucky."

Her eyes widened. The boss. "Good morning, Mrs.
Colby-Camp."

"You must have read my mind," Victoria mused. "I
was about to call for you to come down. I'd like you to
accompany me for an appointment this morning."

"Of course." Lucky's job was all-inclusive when
it came to the needs of Victoria.

A frown pinching her face, Victoria Colby-Camp
glanced past Lucky. Lucky turned to see if someone
else had exited the building. She saw no one.

"Why don't you get in and I'll explain on the
way."

A little confused—but that seemed to be the
theme for the day—Lucky climbed into the limo
next to her boss. "Is everything all right?" Victoria
seemed a little nervous, which was completely out
of character.

"Yes, everything's fine." To the driver, she said,
"I'm ready now."

He turned back to make eye contact with the
woman in charge. "The clinic?"

"Yes." The head of the Colby Agency folded
her hands in her lap, keeping her attention focused
forward.

Clinic? "Are we meeting a client?" Lucky ventured. She was aware that the Colby Agency went out of the way to facilitate the needs of clients, so it seemed a reasonable question. But hadn't Lucas said Victoria was having breakfast with a friend?

Mrs. Colby-Camp turned to face her. "Lucky, you're brand new at the agency. But I trust that what I'm about to tell you will go no further."

Lucky's heart rate jumped back into that crazy, frantic rhythm. "You have my word, ma'am."

The woman Lucky admired so greatly stared forward once more. "I am not one to keep secrets from my husband and my son, but this is for the best."

Her voice sounded distant, wistful. "Is something wrong?" Every cell in Lucky's brain screamed at her that something was very, very wrong.

"Yes." Victoria inhaled a deep, halting breath. "Something is quite wrong."

Sweet heavens. Lucky choked back the worry rising in her throat. "How can I help?"

"There is a treatment that may possibly outmaneuver this disaster," Mrs. Colby-Camp said softly. "It's fairly simple. Only takes an hour or so. I'll know within the week if it's going to work."

That was why they were going to a clinic. Lucky wanted to ask what would happen if it didn't work, but she couldn't bring herself to voice her fears. The need to flat-out ask the nature of the disaster had her pressing her lips firmly together.

"I see no need to put my family through the emotional drama if this simple procedure will take care of things." Victoria stared at her hands a moment. "Still, I wasn't looking forward to going to the clinic alone."

Lucky wanted to reach over and hug her. "I'm glad you thought of me." Victoria looked so desolate, so unlike the strong, powerful woman whose reputation had plowed a famous path all the way to Texas. Lucky had heard the stories about the Colby Agency and she had known that being a part of the agency was what she wanted above all else.

"When the procedure is over," Lucky's boss went on, seeming to gather her courage once more, "we'll return to the office and this will be our secret until such time that it becomes necessary to share the details with my husband and son."

At the mention of Victoria's husband, Lucky thought of the package in her pocket. Lucas was depending on her to deliver it…but this, well, this thing with Victoria took precedence.

Maybe when Mrs. Colby-Camp was settled in for the procedure, Lucky could have the driver run her to the address Lucas had provided. She would be back in plenty of time. Victoria wouldn't even know she'd been gone. Lucky would have accomplished both missions and neither would be the wiser.

That would work.

Lucky sat back in the lush leather seat. She couldn't help stealing a peek at Victoria from the corner of her eyes. She looked so grim. Whatever was wrong it had to be bad. Lucky's mother would say this was a good time to pray.

But Lucky had stopped praying a long time ago. And her mother wasn't exactly a stellar role model.

Funny, for a woman with the name Lucky, she'd never had much luck. Not the good kind anyway.

Maybe Victoria Colby-Camp hadn't had much either. Lucky had heard bits and pieces of the story about her son. Jim Colby had been missing for twenty years when his mother had finally found him. During that same time her first husband had been murdered.

Seemed like the lady could use some good luck herself.

Chapter Three

"One last transaction."

Darnell Raspberry glared up at Dakota from his desk. "Are you insane? Mr. Wallace is going to kill you, but first he'll kill me. I can't keep doing this!"

Dakota slapped the man on the back. "One more," he prompted. "And then I'll be on my way."

Raspberry grumbled something about him being left behind to take the heat. Dakota didn't bother reminding him that was the way it went when a guy chose to live a life of crime. When it was good, it was good, but when things went bad it was generally seriously bad.

Dakota recited the untraceable numbered account for Raspberry, then reached over his shoulder and entered the security code himself.

"Now." Dakota grabbed Raspberry by the collar and hauled him out of his chair. "Let's take a walk."

"But you said you'd go," Raspberry whined. "I did everything you asked!"

"Which way to the men's room?"

Raspberry muttered desperate protests all the way to the men's room. Good thing no one else was expected in the office for another half hour or so.

"Now." Dakota shoved the man into one of the two stalls. "Take off your belt and sit."

Hands shaking, Raspberry removed his belt and crumpled onto the toilet seat.

"Put your knees up and grab your ankles."

The man's eyes rounded in fear, but he obeyed.

Dakota threaded the belt beneath the backs of his knees and then cinched it, essentially squeezing his forearms and legs together. Getting loose wouldn't be difficult, but it would require a balancing act and some finagling and it would give Dakota time to get the hell out of the building.

He patted the guy on the head. "You keep quiet and I won't be back. I hear you yelling and I'm coming to shut you up."

Raspberry nodded, his eyes wild with hysteria.

Dakota checked the corridor then exited the men's room. Two minutes later he was out of the building and leaving the scene at a brisk walk. He'd parked his truck a block away then taken a cab to Raspberry's residence. Planning ahead was the key to a successful mission. Before anyone arrived to find Raspberry wailing at the top of his lungs, Dakota would be long gone.

Once in his truck, he checked the status of the numbered accounts via his smart phone. A grin split across his face. "Oh, yeah. Now that's what I call equalizing."

Every single one of the innocent victims Wallace had cheated now had their money—with interest—in a special account waiting to be claimed.

Dakota peeled off the rubber nose and chin, then the meticulously groomed mustache and sideburns. He scrubbed a hand over his face to rid his skin of the adhesive residue and then started the engine. He shifted into first but before he could let out on the clutch his cell vibrated. Sliding his phone open, he eased out on the clutch and rolled into the street. "Garrett."

"Stellar work, Garrett."

The boss. "All in a day's work." Dakota made the statement with a nonchalance he didn't quite feel. Though he wasn't opposed to roughing up the bad guys, the rest was questionable. No matter that Wallace had stolen from the victims. To Dakota, stealing the money back was also a crime. It reminded him way too much of his mercenary days. And a few other incidents he'd just as soon not recall.

He'd walked away from that life…with good reason.

"I have another job for you."

Surprised, Dakota said, "I'm your man." That was his stock answer. Work was about the only thing going in his life these days, so the more of it the better. But the enigmatic head of the Equalizers had insisted that no one would be allowed to work

back-to-back assignments. The cases brought to the
Equalizers were risky in more ways than one. The
assignments required exacting attention to detail and
unfailing physical readiness. Dakota executed a swift
mental and physical inventory. He was good to go.
As long as he didn't end up in jail, or worse, he had
no problem with jumping right into the next case.

"A young woman will be delivering a package this
morning," Slade Keaton, the overly secretive head of
the Equalizers, explained. No one had even known
his name, much less seen his face until a couple days
ago. "I want you to follow her. Get the identity of the
person who receives the package and report back to
me."

Sounded easy enough. "What about the woman?"
Just how far was Dakota supposed to go to ensure
he accomplished his assignment? Waltzing into an
operation already in progress with no background
details wasn't exactly his favorite dance.

"No contact," Keaton ordered. "I don't want her
to know she's being followed. The delivery is for a
former spook, Lucas Camp. If he gets wind that his
protégée was followed, he'll be trouble."

Lucas Camp. Dakota didn't know the name.
"Who's this Lucas Camp?" Had to be someone significant to an upcoming or ongoing case or Keaton
wouldn't waste time on him. Not that Dakota or
anyone else on staff at the Equalizers knew enough
about their employer to make a reliable assessment.
He merely measured the man by the cases he took

and the orders he doled out. So far Dakota couldn't call him a bad guy, just one who liked to bend and twist the rules.

"He's irrelevant," Keaton said, dismissing Dakota's question. "Report back to me as soon as you have the identity of the person who receives the package. I'm sending a photo of Lucky Malone and her current location to your phone. She'll be making the delivery soon."

"Got it covered." Dakota ended the call. Lucky Malone. The mule, likely nothing more. But this Lucas Camp had to be more no matter that Keaton had played off the question. Dakota checked his phone for the location Keaton sent and headed in that direction.

En route Dakota put in a call to an old contact from his military days.

By the time he reached the clinic where Malone was reported to be, Dakota had the scoop on Lucas Camp. Not just a former spook, the guy was the epitome of what the CIA had once stood for. Dark, dangerous and full of secrets.

This was no casual operation. Keaton was trawling deep, murky waters.

But Dakota had his orders. He parked across the street from the small parking lot fronting the clinic. The clinic was a posh place. Private. No insurance clients seeking treatment at this place. This was where the folks with money went for the caliber of treatment perhaps unobtainable anywhere else.

Malone had to be the daughter of some rich dude. She wasn't old enough to be rich in her own right unless she'd inherited big money. Twenty-five. Five feet, four inches. Coal-black hair and big gray eyes. The chick was a looker and likely had the ego to go with it.

A woman matching Malone's description exited the front entrance. Dakota sat up straighter. He watched as she strode toward a waiting car. It was big and black, though less ostentatious than most limos; nevertheless it left little doubt in regards to the financial portfolio of the backseat's occupant. Malone hesitated at the car door, glanced around as if she feared being watched.

Definitely her.

When she'd settled inside and the car pulled out onto the street, Dakota waited until a full block yawned between them before following. A few turns and twenty-one minutes later and the car stopped at the curb in front of a run-down building. That was the thing about Chicago. One could be in the ritziest part of town and minutes later wander into an area where Mag Mile shoppers wouldn't be caught dead.

Dakota parked half a block back. The street and sidewalks were deserted. To the best of his knowledge, none of the businesses that had once operated along this block as well as two or three around it remained open for commerce. The only tenants were squatters and they would be out and about panhandling for food and money during the daylight hours.

Malone didn't get out of the car right away. If she hadn't been here before, Dakota figured she wasn't too happy about getting out now. While he waited, he used his phone and did a search on her name.

"That's interesting." He divided his attention between the car and his phone. Lucky Malone hailed from Houston. Her family had once been in the oil business but things had gone downhill a number of years back. Lucky had managed to get through college, with major loans, and she'd made her way to Chicago.

But that wasn't the truly interesting part. At seventeen Lucky Malone had been charged with murder. According to the headlines from eight years ago, she'd shot her father in the chest with a twenty-gauge shotgun. The murder rap had later been changed to self-defense and she'd gotten off with only one night in jail. The media had hyped the case to near celebrity status. An alcoholic, abusive husband who beat his wife one time too many stopped by his daughter.

"Damn." Lucky wasn't so lucky after all. Headlines had played up that catch phrase over and over. "Definitely not a lucky lady."

Not by a long shot.

The mother, still alive, resided in a home for the mentally unstable. She'd apparently gone off the deep end after her husband's death.

Malone had no siblings. No close family mentioned.

What she did have was a perfect academic record at the University of Texas.

Malone climbed out of the car. Dakota's attention zeroed in on her. She had a killer body. Even the conservative dress pants couldn't hide a backside like that. The equally modest blouse tightened over nicely rounded breasts as she moved. She said something to the driver before closing the door, then seemed to brace herself before entering the building.

She definitely had something in her hand. Something small and brown.

After another moment's hesitation, she walked up to the door and knocked. The plate-glass door had been boarded up, likely where the glass was missing. She banged on the door a couple of times and nothing happened. Twice she glanced back at the car. Dakota wondered if she were wishing she could jump in and rush away. Strange, a girl who'd had the guts to kill her own daddy shouldn't be afraid of a whole lot.

Finally, she braced both hands on the door and pushed. It didn't budge.

Why would Lucas Camp send her here? Didn't make a whole lot of sense. And what was her connection to Camp? Dakota scanned the area. Maybe the contact would arrive, take the package and split.

Still pushing on the door, Malone stumbled inward, evidently as the ramshackle entrance gave way. Dakota eased the door of his truck open and slid out of the seat. He closed it, careful not to make any more sound than necessary. Considering the driver remained in the car and it was pointed in the other direction, his movements weren't likely to be noticed. With one last look at the building and the car, Dakota hustled to the other end of the alley on his side of the street and double-timed it until he was parallel with the limo.

Careful to stay close against the building on his right, he made his way forward. His position was directly across from the entrance to the building where Malone was to meet her contact.

When he'd come within twelve meters of the parked car, he hung back, watched and listened.

It was quiet, until a low roar brushed against his senses. He went on alert, listened intently. The roar grew louder and louder until a dark sedan skidded to a stop between him and the limo Malone had arrived in.

The sedan's front doors flew open. Two men bailed out and rushed Malone's car. Before the driver had noted the danger or could react, one of the men had dragged him from behind the wheel.

Two unmistakable hisses zipped through the air. Silenced gunshots.

A new kind of tension ignited in Dakota's veins.

A hit team. The driver was dead. Malone and whoever she'd come to meet would be next.

Dakota had palmed his weapon and was stealthily moving around the sedan belonging to the assassins before the two gunmen had made the sidewalk fronting the run-down building Malone had entered.

The second of the two whipped around, his weapon leveled on Dakota.

Too bad he didn't have a silencer.

Dakota dropped the guy before he could pull off a shot.

The other man whirled to fire at him, and Dakota popped him in the center of his forehead.

The gun blasts echoed in the silence. Dakota surveyed the street. Still empty. The stillness resumed, the silence thundered.

Surely someone had heard his shots.

Where the hell were Malone and her contact? They had to have heard the shots.

He started for the entrance to the building when another gunshot rent the air.

This one from inside the building.

Dakota lunged for the door.

Chapter Four

Lucky was intimately acquainted with the smell of blood and the sulfur tinge that filled the air after a gunshot.

The woman, Jennifer, was dead.

As soon as Lucky had identified herself, the woman had said her piece and then she'd stuck the gun she held to her head and pulled the trigger.

Instinctively, Lucky had reached out toward the woman, but she'd been too late to stop what she'd recognized was about to happen.

Even with the better part of the woman's scalp and half her brain splattered on the wall and floor, Lucky had attempted to do something. There was no way to staunch the flow of blood and CPR would be of no use.

There was nothing she could do.

She needed to call for help...to call Lucas.

Lucky sat back on her heels, stared at the blood on her shaking hands. Terror lodged in her throat. Memories slashed through her brain, rendering her incapable of moving. Surely the driver had heard the shots. He would come inside. He would call someone.

The package Lucas had sent lay on the blood-spattered floor. She should pick it up, should make that call, but she couldn't stop staring at the blood.

The woman's last words echoed over and over in Lucky's head, getting all twisted with the old memories she usually kept locked away.

Tell Lucas I can't help him.

What did that mean?

Lucky's gaze stumbled over the brown package again. She picked it up, the blood smearing on the paper wrapping as she turned it over.

She had to call Lucas…someone…

"Hands up, lady."

Lucky pushed to her feet, turning as she did so to face the male voice. She tried to blink away the shock swaddling her brain but it wouldn't be dismissed. She dragged in a breath, even that instinctive movement sluggish. "Who are you?"

"Hands up," he repeated.

Giving herself a mental shake, she slowly lifted her hands. Sweet heavens, she was about to be shot. He held a weapon and it was aimed right at her.

Lucky opened her mouth to scream but nothing came out.

The man came closer.

Maybe he was a cop.

He didn't look like a cop. His hair was too long.

His clothes too fancy. Cops didn't wear business suits on the job, did they?

Maybe a detective. Had someone called the police?

Her heart stuttered to a near stop.

No, he wasn't a cop. The image of the woman lying dead on the dirty floor behind her passed before Lucky's eyes. She swayed, her knees weak.

"Just keep those hands where I can see them."

He patted her down with his free hand. She tried to clear her head and formulate a logical thought. Maybe he was a cop. What did she know about how cops dressed in Chicago? His hand moved around her waist. She should have been offended since she hadn't done anything wrong but she couldn't rally the energy for the reaction. Images of her being arrested all those years ago, the weapon wrenched from her hands, kept intruding on the here and now.

She ordered the memories away.

"I should call the police," she managed to push out past the lump in her throat.

When the man appeared satisfied that she was not armed, he stepped around her and assessed the dead woman on the floor. "Who's this?"

That wasn't the response she'd hoped for. "I am the police" was supposed to be his next comment. She blinked, reminded herself he'd asked a question. "I don't know." Lucky let her hands drop to her sides and he didn't protest. "Jennifer something." She held up the package in her hand. "I was bringing this to her." Lucky shuddered. "She shot herself right in front of me." More of those ugly, too-vivid images from the past invaded the present.

The man with the gun crouched down and took a closer look at the woman, then surveyed the room. When he checked the dead woman's pockets, Lucky snapped out of the coma she'd lapsed into.

"What're you doing?" For God's sake the woman was dead! If he wasn't a cop, he shouldn't be tampering with the body.

"Trying to determine her identity," he said without slowing from his work.

"Won't the police do that?" Who was this man? Better question, why wasn't she running? He could be a killer for all she knew.

He pulled something from his pocket. Ice slid through her veins. A cell phone. She sagged with relief. He snapped a couple of pictures of the victim then pushed to his feet.

Lucky stared at him, her mouth gaping. Who was this man?

"You should probably get out of here," he suggested as he slid his phone back into his pocket, then started for the door.

Was he insane? "I can't just leave! I have to call the police." She needed her purse, her cell phone. Why hadn't she brought either inside with her? Both were still in the car.

"I wouldn't hang around," he warned, pausing

at the door. "Those guys may have friends on the way."

What was he talking about? Her face scrunched in confusion. "What guys?"

He raised his eyebrows. "Are you deaf? The ones who killed your driver."

"That's not possible. I…" Lucky didn't finish her protest. She ran past him, bolting out the door onto the sidewalk where yet another bloody scene waited.

The body of a stranger lay across the sidewalk in her path. Horrified, she edged around it and rushed around to the driver's side of the car she'd arrived in. The driver lay on the ground, blood all around his head.

Her chest cramped. What was happening? Who would do this?

Another man she couldn't identify lay on the street a few feet away.

Judging from the volume of blood, he was dead, too.

She whirled to face the man who, very much alive, waited a few steps behind her. "Who are you?"

"The man who just saved your life." He shoved the weapon into the waistband of his jeans. "An old-fashioned thank-you would be nice."

Lucky shook her head. This guy was crazy…she was crazy. Why was she standing here? "I need my phone." She walked around the blockade that her self-proclaimed savior made and then grimaced when forced to step around the driver's body. A shudder quaked through her. This was wrong…crazy. How had this happened?

She opened the rear door of the car and reached inside for her purse. Behind her, the man who claimed to have rescued her was snapping more photos with his cell. Why would he do that? Was he some kind of private investigator? A criminal? Obviously he had no compunction about killing.

Four people were dead. The man who'd done at least part of the killing was right behind her. She needed help.

Her hands shook as she fished in her bag for the phone. The man stopped snapping pictures and said, "Garrett."

Lucky glanced over her shoulder. He'd answered his cell. His name was Garrett.

Focus, Lucky. She turned back to her task. She had to call 9-1-1 first…or call Lucas?

Victoria.

The air rushed out of Lucky's lungs. She'd left Mrs. Colby-Camp at the clinic.

"Oh, God." She fiddled with the phone, slid it open and hit 9.

"We gotta go."

She drew her upper body out of the car and glared at the man. "What?"

Before Lucky could comprehend his intent, the man—Garrett—grabbed her by the arm and started hauling her away from the car.

"What're you doing?" She jerked at his hold. "I have to call—"

"What you have to do, lady, is get out of here before more trouble arrives."

Fear exploded in her chest. She twisted to see one end of the block, then the other. "No one's coming."

"Yet," he qualified.

He stopped at a blue truck and opened the driver's-side door.

Reality crashed into Lucky.

This man was kidnapping her.

"Let me go!" She yanked against his hold. He buried his fingers into her skin that much more deeply.

"Not until I've gotten you out of danger."

"I will press charges, sir," she shouted, her voice quavering pathetically. What had he said? Get her out of danger?

"Whatever." He grabbed her around the waist and lifted her into the truck on the driver's side. "Now scoot over and buckle up."

As soon as he'd released her she scrambled for the passenger-side door.

Strong fingers tangled in the back of her blouse. "Not so fast." He pulled her around to face him. "Buckle up." He withdrew his weapon with his left hand, but kept the barrel pointed upward. "Or else."

Lucky grabbed the seat belt and pulled it into

place. When the fastener clicked, the man started the engine and roared away from the curb.

She forced herself to think. Had he actually rescued her or had he killed those other people to get to her? She shook her head. That didn't make sense. She was nobody. Why would he want to kidnap her? Not to mention that woman, Jennifer, had committed suicide right in front of Lucky. This guy had had nothing to do with that. He hadn't even been in the room.

What in the world was all this about?

All she knew was that Jennifer was Mr. Camp's contact.

Tell Lucas I can't help him.

Lucky had to get that message to Mr. Camp. He would know what to do. What was she thinking? It didn't take a master's degree in criminal procedure to know she needed to call the police.

"We can't leave the scene like this," she said. Her voice shook as badly as the rest of her. Adrenaline, she realized. The panic was crowding in, mixed with a little shock. Maybe the shock was already hindering her ability to react rationally.

Her self-proclaimed savior appeared too busy with driving like a bat out of hell and keeping a watch on his rearview mirror to respond.

"I said," she repeated, louder this time, "we can't just leave like this. We have to call the police."

"You can call whoever you want to," he tossed

back at her without so much as a glance, "as soon as I drop you off."

"Drop me off?" He was letting her go? Relief crowded into her chest. "Where?"

"The agency where you work." He braked at an intersection, rolled forward enough to check the cross street and then vaulted forward.

Thank God. She relaxed marginally. Leaving the scene was still against the law, but at least she would be back at the office where she could get help. The police would understand that she had been forced to leave. She hadn't done so of her own—

Victoria.

"Wait."

He hit the brakes. A horn blew behind them. "What?"

"I have to go back to the clinic." He'd have no idea what she was talking about, but that didn't matter. She rattled off the address. "Hurry!"

"Why do you want to go back there?" He shouldered out of the fancy suit jacket as if he had all day and wasn't blocking one entire side of the street.

The frustrated driver in the car behind them whipped past, blew the horn again and shouted some profanity out his window.

Lucky held up both hands and closed her eyes a moment to clear her head. She had to pull herself together here. "I left my boss at the clinic this morning for a procedure. I was supposed to stay until she was ready to leave, but I had this delivery to make."

Where was the package? She looked around, saw it in the floor. At least she hadn't lost it during all that insanity. But her purse...she'd left it in the car.

"She can call a cab." He let out on the clutch and stamped the accelerator, rocketing forward.

"You don't understand!" Lucky turned fully in the seat to face him fully. "Please. I can't just leave her there." The promise she'd made to Victoria haunted Lucky now. "I have to be there for her. I can't go back to the office without her."

The man plowed the fingers of one hand through his hair. "Fine. It's on the way anyhow."

Lucky fell back against the seat. What in God's name had just happened? She was going to be in big trouble for leaving Mrs. Colby-Camp, for failing to deliver Mr. Camp's package and for leaving the scene of a crime.

She stole a glance at the driver. Leaving with the shooter of at least two of the victims had to make her actions even more criminal.

Dear God, she was so screwed.

And those people were so dead.

She told herself to get as many of the facts as possible. "Your name is Garrett?"

"That's right."

"And you witnessed those two men kill the driver?"

"I did. They dragged him out of the car and shot him on the spot. They were headed inside after you when I interceded."

Wait. A frown furrowed across her brow, emphasizing the ache of tension there. "How did you know I was in the building?"

He said nothing.

"Do you live in the area?" she demanded. Not very likely since several of the blocks appeared not only run-down but abandoned.

Still he didn't answer.

"Were you waiting for your connection?" Frustration and anger kicked aside the hysteria. "Or waiting to make some illegal deal?" Fury chased away the more fragile emotions.

"I don't buy, sell or use drugs, lady."

Then she knew. "You were following me!" For the life of her she couldn't imagine why, but that had to be the case. Or maybe he'd followed Mr. Camp's contact.

He made a hard left, pitching her around.

She righted herself, shoved the hair out of her eyes. "That's what you were doing, isn't it?"

He said nothing. He didn't have to. It was true. He had been following her or the woman, Jennifer. He had to be connected to her delivery for Mr. Camp. Whatever she did now, Lucky had to commit to memory every detail about this man. Mr. Camp would want to know. The police would want to know. She didn't dare attempt getting a picture with her cell phone. Wait…where was her cell? She covertly checked her pockets but didn't dare check the floorboard in case she'd dropped it. He did have a gun and clearly he wasn't shy about using it.

He was tall. At least a head taller than her, maybe six feet or a little more. Sandy-colored hair. Brown eyes. Square jaw. Broad shoulders. Muscular, but not heavy. Lean. He'd rolled up the sleeves of the white button-down shirt he wore, revealing a couple of tattoos. She didn't recognize the symbol on his right forearm and couldn't see the one on the left well enough to make out details.

When he let her out at the clinic she could attempt to get his license plate number as he drove away.

The truck came to an abrupt stop. Lucky swung her attention to the street. The clinic. Relief washed over her. Thank God.

"You can give the police my description," he said, jerking her attention back to him. "But it won't do you any good."

She held her breath, kept her gaze steady on his as she slowly reached for the door handle. "Why is that, Mr. Garrett?"

"I'm not in any databases. I'm nowhere." He leaned toward her and she gasped. "I don't exist, Ms. Malone."

He had been following her! How else would he know her name?

"Now skedaddle."

Lucky wrenched the door open and practically fell face-forward onto the street. The truck sat really high off the ground. She scrambled to her feet and rushed to the clinic entrance. Once inside, she would check on Victoria, borrow a phone to call 9-1-1 and then call Mr. Camp.

Breathless, she checked the waiting room for a bathroom. Relief gushed through her when she spotted the door. She hurried across the deserted waiting room and closed herself in the tiny room. Her hands shook as she turned on the faucet and then pumped a palm full of soap. Lucky scrubbed hard, memories she didn't want to recall swarming her brain. She banished the haunting mental images and dried her hands. After a swipe of her left cheek she checked her blouse. Red spots stained the fabric. Nothing she could do about that. She buttoned her jacket—it was too dark for any blood splatters to show. Exiting the bathroom, she walked straight to the reception desk.

She closed her eyes for a second and searched for calm. Maybe she'd finally gone as crazy as her mother. Maybe she had imagined all of the past hour.

"May I help you?"

Lucky opened her eyes. The woman behind the desk peered up at her with blatant annoyance despite the cheery pink scrubs she wore.

"I'd like to check on Victoria Colby-Camp." Lucky took a much-needed breath and ordered herself to calm down. She would get through this.

The woman flipped through her appointment book, then riffled through the files and papers on her desk. She shook her head.

Lucky's stomach dropped into the vicinity of her thrift store shoes. She was too late.

"I'm sorry," the woman finally said. "We don't have a patient by that name."

What? Stay calm, she told herself. "She may have left already," Lucky suggested. "She came in an hour or so ago for a procedure." Lucky leaned forward, glanced pointedly at the appointment book. "Victoria Colby-Camp. She must be on there. I brought her here myself."

"Let me check to see if her paperwork is still in back." The receptionist stepped away from her desk, disappearing into the corridor that led to the treatment rooms.

Lucky maintained her position at the counter, her heart thundering, denial raging through her. How could all of this have happened in such a short time?

The woman in the pink scrubs came back shaking her head. Her curly blond locks swung with the action. "I'm sorry, there must be some mistake. No one has spoken to or treated a Victoria Colby-Camp. She's not on our schedule for today and she's not here." She shrugged. "She isn't a patient of this clinic."

The room suddenly closed in on Lucky. Fear clamped hard around her chest. "That's not possible. I brought her here…watched her check in."

"Are you certain it was this clinic?" the receptionist asked. "There are several others within a four- or five-block radius."

"Of course I'm sure." Lucky locked her knees to prevent them from giving way. Wrong, wrong, wrong! This was wrong!

"I don't know what to tell you, ma'am."

Wait, maybe she'd used another name. Victoria had said she didn't want anyone to know. "She may have used a different name." Lucky rattled off her boss's description.

She had to be back there, assuming Victoria hadn't left already.

"I'm sorry," the receptionist said, "no one matching that description has been in this morning."

Impossible. "Thank you. I must have made a mistake."

The receptionist turned her attention back to her work. Lucky bolted for the double doors leading into the clinic proper. The receptionist yelled something but Lucky didn't slow down. She burst into the first room she encountered. A woman wearing a hospital gown gasped.

The doctor swung his attention from his patient to Lucky and demanded, "What's going on here?"

Lucky could hear the woman in the pink scrubs calling for security, but Lucky just kept rushing from room to room. She checked the next room, and the next. One was empty; another was occupied with what appeared to be another doctor and his patient.

In a dead run now, Lucky pushed through the double doors into the surgery area.

But that was as far as she got.

Two uniformed gorillas grabbed her and dragged her back to the lobby.

"Consider yourself fortunate that I'm not calling the police," pink scrubs lady said. "Now, go home and take your medication. You're clearly delusional."

When Lucky would have balked, the two uniformed men crowded closer, forcing her to back up against the front entrance of the lobby.

"Out," one of them ordered.

Lucky turned around and pushed out the door.

In a daze, she ambled across the parking lot. She had to call Mr. Camp.

She stared down at herself. Where was her phone? The package? The need to crumble into an impotent heap overwhelmed her. She felt her pockets again. How had she lost her phone?

The blue truck that had brought her here suddenly rolled to a stop on the street in front of her. The passenger-side window slowly rolled down.

"You left this." The driver held up the blood-stained package.

Lucky gathered her courage, barely holding back the tears, and walked over to the truck. She reached inside and accepted the package. "Thank you." Her lips quivered in spite of her best efforts to maintain her composure.

"What's wrong?"

What was she waiting for? All she had to do was borrow a phone. Call the agency. Call 9-1-1. Report the shootings.

Report her boss missing.

Lucky Malone was in big trouble here.

This whole morning was... There were no adequate words to describe it.

"My boss is missing."

"This Victoria Colby-Camp you've been talking about?" he asked.

She nodded, a sob tearing at her throat.

He leaned across the seat and pushed the door open. "Get in. I'll take you wherever you need to go."

It was in that instant—that pivotal moment—that Lucky realized what she had to do.

She moved her head side to side. "No."

Garrett frowned. She hadn't known him very long but she was pretty sure she saw sympathy in his eyes.

"I can't go back without her."

Skepticism replaced the sympathy. "How's that?"

Lucky pointed to the clinic. "I left her here. Something happened while I was gone and now the people inside are saying she was never here. That's a lie. They're covering up something. They've kidnapped her or..." She couldn't even think about the other possibility. "I have to find her."

Lucky was pretty sure she had just stepped off the

deep end. What she had just said to this guy sounded crazy.

She stepped back from the truck. "Thank you for your offer of help. But I can't go anywhere until I figure this out."

Garrett looked away a moment. He was the one shaking his head now.

Didn't matter. This wasn't about him. Lucky had to figure out how to do this.

Her boss had made her promise not to tell about coming to the clinic. She had to try and protect that promise. The only way to do that was to find Victoria without telling anyone else.

Lucky closed her eyes. That was even crazier than all the other insane events of the morning. She was a part of a homicide—a triple homicide. Calling the police was way overdue. She'd clearly suffered some sort of emotional breakdown.

"Well," Garrett said, drawing her attention back to him, "I hope you find her."

Lucky managed a jerky nod. Speaking was out of the question. If she opened her mouth again, the sobs would escape.

Instead, she stood there and watched the stranger drive away.

And she prayed.

Chapter Five

Dakota told himself to keep driving. That the lady's problems were not his.

He glanced in the rearview mirror one last time, her image growing smaller and smaller with every turn of the wheels. But no amount of distance could exile from his head the fear he'd seen in her eyes, the desperation he'd heard in her voice.

"Damn." He braked to a stop at the curb and fished his cell phone from his pocket.

Whatever stupid step he took next, he had to inform his boss. Not that he was slated for any other assignments just now, but with Keaton one never knew what he'd come up with. Like today's crazy surveillance duty.

His boss's voice followed the first ring. "Keaton."

"We have a problem." Dakota had already explained to his boss about the ambush at the delivery point and his necessary actions. Killing two people, even in self-defense, and then leaving the scene was not exactly within the boundaries of the law.

But getting dragged through a homicide investigation was the last thing his boss wanted. Dakota had forwarded to Keaton the pictures he'd taken of the victims. The reason, like the man, was a complete mystery to Dakota. Keaton had assured Dakota that he had high-level contacts within the Chicago P.D. and he would see that Dakota's account of the event was passed along to the proper channels.

"I dropped the lady off like you said but she didn't want to go to the agency. She wanted to be taken to a clinic," he explained. In their previous conversation, Keaton had insisted that the woman, Lucky Malone, could not be left at the scene for any reason. Enemies of Lucas Camp, according to Keaton, were like roaches. Where you saw one or two there were plenty more. And they would not want to leave loose ends. "But she's all hysterical at the moment because the clinic appears to have lost her boss."

"What?"

Something that sounded far too much like shock echoed in the one word. Couldn't be. Nothing fazed Slade Keaton. "Malone says she left Victoria Colby-Camp at the clinic before going to make the drop for Lucas Camp. Now the staff claims the woman was never at the clinic. Like I said, Malone's hysterical. What—"

"Find Victoria Colby-Camp." Keaton's voice was ice cold now, void of the shock or whatever Dakota had thought he'd heard. "Now."

Dakota blinked. That was his plan, sort of. He

couldn't leave Malone back there. Not and sleep any-time soon. But the missing woman had an entire P.I. agency that could look for her. Why was Keaton so interested in her whereabouts? "I'll check the place out and see what I can learn."

"Listen to me, Garrett," Keaton ordered. "I don't care what you have to do, who you have to kill. Find Victoria. Now. I want an update every hour. I want to know who is responsible for this. Whatever you do, don't let Malone check in with her agency."

"She's not going to go for that," Dakota protested. "She has—"

"Tell her Lucas sent you to protect her in the event of trouble. She is to lay low until the dust settles since what she witnessed has no doubt made her a target. She is to stay dark until he orders otherwise. As soon as I have something on the clinic I will con-tact you."

Before Dakota could protest again, his boss sev-ered the connection. Dakota stared at the phone. "What the…?" He shook his head, shoved the phone back into his pocket and muttered, "No problem."

He didn't mind taking back-to-back cases. Money was money. But this whole whacked-out scenario was off the charts.

After checking the mirrors, he executed a three-point turn and headed back in Malone's direction. She stood right where he'd left her. He leaned across the seat and opened the passenger door. "Get in."

She looked at him, those big gray eyes still filled with terror. "I can't leave. I told you that already."

"Just get in." He shrugged and threw up his hands. "We'll figure this out." He surveyed the front of the clinic. "You keep standing around out here and they'll call the cops."

Malone glanced over her shoulder, then reluctantly climbed into the truck.

"You call anyone and report what happened?" If they were about to have company he'd like to know.

"No. I…didn't have my cell. I must have dropped it." She shook her head, her face pinched with confusion. "I think I'm in shock."

Dakota drove around the block, then pulled into a slot behind a row of parked cars in the lot directly across from the clinic. He exhaled a resigned breath. "Start at the beginning. Tell me everything that happened."

Malone sat there a moment, evidently pulling herself together. "This morning as I was leaving the agency to make a delivery for Mr. Camp, Mrs. Colby-Camp asked me to accompany her to an appointment."

"At this clinic?" Dakota jerked his head toward the sleek upscale building across the street.

His passenger nodded. "She didn't want anyone at the agency to know. Especially not her husband."

"Lucas Camp?"

Malone nodded.

Interesting. "So you came here with her and the driver?"

"Yes. I was…" Malone's voice quavered and she had to start again. "I was supposed to wait in the lobby while she had the procedure." She shrugged listlessly. "But Mr. Camp wanted me to make that delivery. I figured I could take care of that and be back before the procedure was completed. Now she's missing." Malone covered her face with her hands. "I shouldn't have left her here. I should have told Mr. Camp I couldn't make his delivery."

Dakota glanced at the small package protruding from her pocket. "What exactly did the clinic staff say?" Hell, this Victoria could have discovered Malone gone with the driver and car and called someone else to pick her up. She might not be missing at all.

Malone cleared her throat. "They claim they have had no patient by that name or matching her description. When I insisted I'd brought her here they said I was delusional."

A frown nagged at Dakota's brow. "Did you call the office to see if maybe your boss changed her mind about the procedure and just left?"

Malone shook her head. "I guess I should have used the clinic's phone and checked before I got hysterical."

Dakota pulled out his cell. "What's the office number?"

Malone looked confused.

"It won't hurt to check before we jump to conclusions."

Malone provided the numbers. According to the Colby Agency receptionist, Victoria wasn't in her office this morning. She wasn't at home and didn't answer her cell. Not good.

"We might be able to track her movements via her cell phone," he offered.

More confusion cluttered Malone's face. "You can do that with your personal cell phone?"

"I have resources." Dakota entered the number into a text and forwarded it to his boss with a request to attempt a triangulation of the cell phone's location. If the cell remained on, there was a chance it could be tracked.

How had this Malone chick gotten a job with a group like the Colby Agency? Clearly she didn't know her way around this business. Talk about inexperienced and ill prepared for the job. Giving her grace, he admitted that this had been a tough one, even for a seasoned investigator.

"We can't just sit here," Malone said, her attention focused on the clinic. "We have to do something."

"What we're going to do is see who comes and goes until we have a starting place beyond this ritzy clinic." He glanced at his phone though he hadn't felt it vibrate. The sooner he had a location on the missing woman's cell, the better.

Malone put up her hands. "I can't do this. The promise I made to keep this visit to the clinic a se-

cret is irrelevant now. I have to call Mr. Camp." She
glanced wistfully at Dakota's cell. "Can I use your
phone?"

Dakota couldn't put off the next step any longer.
"It's time for you to know the truth." When she stared
up at him with that panicked expression that made
him wish he hadn't been dragged into this, he gave
her the story he'd been ordered to tell. "Lucas sent me
to keep an eye on you while you made the delivery…
in the event there was trouble."

Surprise, then doubt and ultimately total confusion
played out on her face. "Why didn't you tell me that
in the first place?" She closed her eyes and blew out
a ragged breath. "Thank God."

Definitely a newbie. She'd swallowed the story
without so much as a hiccup.

"He knows about Victoria…?" Malone turned to
him again, searched his eyes. "Are they trying to find
her?" Renewed worry clouded her eyes.

Dakota's cell vibrated, saving him from having to
come up with an answer on that one. He checked the
screen. A text from Keaton.

The phone is in the clinic.

Another message advised that the coordinates
were being downloaded to Dakota's phone. A street
map appeared on the screen with a red dot repre-
senting the position of the cell phone belonging to
Victoria Colby-Camp.

"He does know, doesn't he?" Malone bit her lip
and mumbled, "Oh, God."

"The situation," Dakota offered, "is extremely sensitive. There are certain precautions that have to be taken." That didn't answer her question. He hoped she wouldn't notice.

"Why aren't they here?" She craned her neck to check the street. "What about the police? I'm certain they would've called the police. This is crazy." She plowed her fingers through her hair. "Just crazy."

Dakota hoped he wasn't backing himself into a corner. "There's a strong possibility that Victoria's disappearance is related to the same people who ambushed you this morning." He hadn't been advised of any sort of explanation, leaving him no other alternative. "As I said, the situation has to be approached with extreme caution. Your orders are to lay low until the situation is resolved." All Dakota needed was for her to agree to allow him to park her some place out of the way until this was done. Whatever the hell *this* was.

Malone shook her head adamantly. "I can't do that! This is my fault! I should never have left her!" She gestured to Dakota, then to the clinic. "You have a gun. You could make them tell us the truth."

A new level of desperation had set in. "Yeah," he grunted, "and we could both end up in jail. How would we help your boss then? Not to mention Lucas would have my hide," he remembered to add.

Defeat pressed down her shoulders. "I don't know." She dropped her head against the seat. "I don't know anything. This is only my second week on the job."

Damn. He had known she was a newbie, but surely an agency as elite as the Colby Agency wouldn't hire someone this green as an investigator. "What exactly do you do at the agency?"

She turned her head just far enough to look at him. "I'm an assistant to Mrs. Colby-Camp. Mr. Camp has to know this is my fault."

Dakota's cell vibrated. He stared at the map on the screen. "They're moving."

"What?" Malone leaned across the seat to look at the screen.

An ambulance rounded the corner of the clinic, eased into the street and rolled away.

Dakota started his truck and backed out of the slot.

"What's happening?" Malone demanded.

"Assuming your boss is with her phone," he said as he edged between two parked vehicles to reach the street in the most direct route, "she's in that ambulance." Careful to keep his distance, Dakota followed the white vehicle.

"Oh, my God." Malone eased forward in her seat. "They are kidnapping her."

"Looks that way." Dakota didn't like it one bit that he didn't have a clue what was going down. But he had his orders. Find Victoria Colby-Camp.

"Shouldn't you call Mr. Camp?"

Logical question. Dakota flashed his cell at her. "He's receiving the same intel."

That seemed to satisfy her for the moment.

The ambulance appeared to be moving away from the city. Dakota placed his phone on the dash and focused on the vehicle half a block ahead. Traffic helped, but it wouldn't last if the ambulance continued on its present course.

He had grown up in Chicago. For the past year he'd called the Windy City home once more. Exactly why remained a mystery to him. He'd sworn when he left more than a decade ago that he would never return. There was nothing here for him. But then he'd gotten this job offer and he'd thought what the hell.

"Where are they going?" Malone asked as she peered out the windshield. "I don't know anything about this side of Chicago." She turned to Dakota. "We're leaving the city, aren't we?"

"Looks that way."

Once they left the city limits behind, he fell back a few more car lengths. As long as he wasn't spotted he had the advantage. The miles and the minutes ticked off, five, then ten. Twenty, then thirty. Where the hell were they headed? He studied the landscape. A bad, bad feeling had started deep in his gut.

Malone started pawing around in the glove box and then the floorboard. She tugged at the buttons of her jacket evidently for better mobility. She bent down and groped around under the seat.

He glanced at her twice, recognizing the signs of renewed hysteria. "What're you looking for?"

"I have to get this blood off." She stared at her stained blouse now. "And I can't find my phone."

The ambulance took a left onto a county road. The route was vaguely familiar to Dakota. He'd been this way before. He just couldn't remember when or why.

"I should've called the police." Malone gave up on her search. "I don't know what I was thinking. That would have been the logical thing to do."

Dakota tuned out her ranting, his full attention zeroed in on the route. The trees…the houses that grew more and more sparse.

Brake lights flashed as the ambulance slowed for a right turn. Once the turn was made the vehicle had disappeared from sight by the time Dakota copied the turn. The road narrowed. The tree line on either side of the road was denser now, broken only by the occasional modest home.

He knew this place somehow.

He slowed as the road climbed a slight rise and then cut sharply to the right. A rusty road sign warned there was no outlet. Once he'd made the bend, he slammed on the brakes.

Malone bumped the dash. "Why are we stopping?"

Dakota couldn't respond.

He went utterly still as full recognition materialized in his brain.

"I know this place."

Hearing the words echo in the silent cab shook him. He hadn't meant to say them out loud.

"You do?"

He blinked. This couldn't be possible.

"What is this place?" Malone demanded. She now stared at the looming structure that waited ominously at the end of the road.

The twelve-foot stone wall stretched out on either side of a main entrance. Iron gates loomed at that entrance, flanked by a guard shack.

Beyond the wall stood a four-story monstrosity that should have burned to the ground decades ago.

"Garrett?"

No way. This couldn't be right.

"What is this place?" Malone repeated.

He turned to his passenger. Her eyes were wide with worry. She had no idea, couldn't possibly have even an inkling, what they'd stumbled into. Who was this Victoria Colby-Camp that she could drag him into the deepest, darkest recesses of his own personal nightmare?

"Garrett," she pressed, "where are they taking her?"

He turned back to the place where the road dead-ended. He hadn't fully recognized the route because he'd only ever gotten glimpses through the rear windows of ambulance doors. He could give Malone the official business name. Flashes from the distant past slashed across his vision. He knew from personal experience exactly what this place was and the name was merely a facade just like the building and the endless wall that surrounded it.

A fear he hadn't suffered in a dozen years swelled

inside him, forced his heart to ram against his sternum and prevented the possibility of a decent breath.

"It's hell, Malone. This place is hell."

Chapter Six

12:00 p.m.

Lucas was worried.

Both Simon and Ian had already asked if he'd heard from Victoria.

Lucas tried her cell yet again.

Voice mail. It could be on silent or perhaps she simply didn't hear the subtle ring tone. Either way, it wasn't like Victoria to be out touch like this.

He tried the driver's cell again.

Then Lucky's.

No answer on either.

Lucas pushed out of the chair behind his desk and moved to the window. Who was the friend Victoria had gone to coffee with this morning? He tried to recall if she'd mentioned a name. Gretchen? Betsy? He just couldn't remember.

Lucas shook his head. How could he forget something as simple as that? He put through another call. Mildred Ballard, Victoria's personal assistant and closest friend, answered immediately.

"Good afternoon, Lucas."

At least someone was answering his calls. "Mildred, how's the makeover going?"

She laughed, one of those uncharacteristically girly sounds. "My hair is gorgeous. I'm stunned that even an old broad like me can still be dolled up. The manicure and pedicure are in process as we speak. It was so sweet of you and Victoria to think of this."

"I can't take credit," Lucas said, trying to be patient. "It's all Victoria's doing."

Mildred delightedly rambled on about how she'd found a gift card in her purse for her favorite department store, so shopping was next.

"Mildred," Lucas interrupted, "I know this is a day off and you're having a wonderful time, but do you know who Victoria was having coffee with this morning?"

Silence thickened on the other end of the line. Though Lucas had attempted to infuse nonchalance in his tone, Mildred knew him too well.

"Has something happened?" The background noise abruptly stopped as if Mildred had lifted a single hand and all in the salon had fallen silent.

"Well…" Lucas managed a dry chuckle. "I had hoped Victoria and I could have lunch but she hasn't come into the office as of yet. I thought I'd give her a call and—"

"Penelope Lewis," Mildred cut in. "They were having coffee at The Broken Egg. Victoria said she'd be in the office well before noon."

Lucas made a mental note of the name and location. "Thank you, Mildred. I'm sure she'll show at any moment."

"Lucky can find Penelope's number for you," Mildred offered. "All Victoria's personal contacts are in the Rolodex on her desk."

"That'll work," Lucas assured her. "Enjoy your day, Mildred." Mildred was right, except Lucky hadn't returned either and she wasn't answering her cell.

Lucas was already halfway to Victoria's office when he slid the cell back into his pocket. His instincts were on point. Something was wrong. He could feel it.

"Lucas."

He hesitated at Victoria's door and waited for Ian Michaels to catch up with him. Ian's expression was most always indecipherable so he tried not to read too much into the seemingly grim look on his face now. "Yes, Ian?" Anxiety niggled at his composure. Something was definitely very wrong.

"Jim and Simon are en route to the location now, but," Ian said, indicating with a gesture of his hand that they should continue on into Victoria's office, "I received a rather disturbing call from the Chicago P.D. a few moments ago. Have you heard from Lucky this morning?"

Lucas stopped in the middle of Victoria's office, that sense of dread mounting at a breath-stealing rate.

"Jim and Simon are en route where?" Ian had skipped right over that part. Lucas braced for bad news.

"You've had no word from Lucky?" Ian asked again, once more ignoring Lucas's question.

Lucas reached for patience. "I asked her to run an errand for me this morning. She should have been back by now. I didn't get an answer when I called her cell."

Worry flickered in Ian's dark eyes. "Burt, Victoria's driver, has been murdered. His body, as well as those of three other victims, was discovered less than an hour ago."

Fear ignited in Lucas's veins. "Victoria?"

"No sign of Victoria."

Lucas reached for his cell. "Where did this happen?" He entered Victoria's number for the umpteenth time as he spoke.

Ian gave the address, stopping Lucas cold.

"You're certain?" Icy terror clamped around his throat.

Ian nodded. "Two of the other victims are male and appeared to be an ambush team of some sort. The detective in charge of the case believes one of the two is responsible for the driver's death judging by the caliber of the weapon used and the positioning of the vehicle in which the ambush team arrived. Jim believes whoever took down the ambush team may have taken Victoria."

"There's been no ransom demand?" Lucas couldn't breathe. "No calls whatsoever?" Of course there hadn't been. He would have been notified immediately.

"Nothing," Ian confirmed.

Something Ian had said in the beginning bobbed to the surface of the sheer terror swimming around in Lucas's brain. "You said there were three victims besides the driver. What about the third one?"

"It's a woman. Jennifer Ashton."

The room shifted and Lucas suddenly wished for the cane he'd used for so many years.

Ian took hold of his arm and steadied him. "We shouldn't think the worst yet. Victoria is a resourceful woman. I'm certain she had a good reason for going to that address."

The address—the one Lucas had been given by his contact—was a crime-infested area. Generally the area was safe in the daylight hours. It was only at night that trouble crept out of its hiding places. He'd sent Lucky there. Had felt certain she'd be safe so early in the morning. Clearly he'd been wrong.

Lucas needed to sit down. For more than thirty years he had been unshakable. Untouchable. Now he felt as weak as a kitten. "I know the address," he said as he collapsed into the nearest chair. "Jennifer Ashton is—was—a contact I've known for years."

"Victoria had business with this contact?" Ian asked, settling into a chair next to Lucas.

Lucas shook his head. "I don't know why she would have gone there. She didn't know about the delivery." His gaze locked with Ian's. "Lucky was going to make the delivery for me. She was to take a taxi and meet Jennifer." Where the hell was Lucky? How had Victoria ended up with her? Lucky was an unknown—none of Lucas's or Victoria's enemies would have been on the watch for. He had been so sure she would be safe. But Victoria... She was a high-profile target for anyone seeking revenge or a fast buck.

Ian reached into his pocket and withdrew his ringing cell phone. "Michaels."

That paralyzing fear pressed in around Lucas once more. Had he caused this horror? None of this was about Victoria and it certainly wasn't about Lucky, now they were both unaccounted for.

"I understand," Ian said to his caller. "Keep me posted."

When he'd put away his phone, he said, "That was Simon. The driver's GPS had been turned off and he made no notes in his activity journal."

"Why would Victoria ask him to keep their movements off the record?" It didn't make sense to Lucas, and he knew Victoria was the only one with the authority to make that request. Burt Cox had been with the Colby Agency for the past two years, since the former driver was killed in an attempt to abduct Victoria's grandchild. Cox had passed the agency's every security check. But that didn't mean they hadn't missed something. The technology for creating a past as well as a present was an ever-changing field.

Even the best couldn't always keep up with the latest techniques.

"Are you at liberty to disclose the nature of the delivery Lucky was to make to Jennifer Ashton?"

Lucas ignored the ache in his right leg, the one he'd lost three decades ago as a prisoner of war. He hadn't suffered that phantom pain in a very long time. Just an indication of how badly the situation had shaken him.

"It's Keaton." Lucas had kept this nagging suspicion to himself for months now.

"The man who took over the Equalizers?" Surprise was evident in Ian's voice.

Lucas nodded. "I had reservations about this anonymous buyer all along, but it wasn't until Victoria and I bumped into him at dinner that those reservations turned to true concern."

"I was under the impression no one had met him," Ian countered. "Not even Jim."

"That's true." Lucas had learned by accident himself. "Victoria and I were at dinner a few days ago and we ran into Maggie James. She introduced her dinner companion as Slade Keaton." For clarification, Lucas added, "That was before Jim learned his identity. There was something about the man. I couldn't quite nail it, but I sensed all through dinner that he paid far too much attention to Victoria and me."

"Maggie from across the street?" Ian confirmed.

"Yes." Maggie James's coffee house was a mainstay of the Mag Mile and was located directly across the street from the Colby Agency. "I've been looking into Keaton since." If he'd put Victoria in danger—or Lucky... Lucas didn't want to believe that. No one was better at covert intelligence gathering. Keaton couldn't possibly know Lucas was checking up on him.

"Have you learned anything that would suggest Keaton is a threat to Victoria or this agency?"

"I've learned nothing," Lucas admitted, a first for him. "Keaton is a ghost in a very real sense of the word. The name only goes back a few years and prior to that it's as if he didn't exist. I've hit a brick wall with every avenue I've chosen to pursue."

Ian, of all people, understood precisely how profound that statement was.

"What about Jennifer Ashton? Her role in your investigation was what?"

Lucas rubbed at his right thigh. The pain seemed to radiate all the way down to his ankle, which was impossible since nothing other than the prosthetic he used existed from just above the knee. "As I said, I've known Jennifer for years. Twenty to be exact. She's a bridge walker. Was a bridge walker," he amended once more with heavy regret.

"She walks in both worlds," Ian clarified.

Lucas agreed with a nod. Jennifer Ashton had been a reliable contact between the sources who operated outside the law and those who upheld the law. She'd provided invaluable information to Lucas many times in the past. And she had a penchant for jewels. Whenever he wanted information, he exchanged her latest must-have jewelry request for her insights. "She contacted me. With numerous resources of her own, she often screens intelligence for anything market-able. She insisted that she had discovered Keaton's true identity and that the information would be of significant interest to me."

"She was prepared to trade this information to you this morning?" Ian didn't have to ask about the price. He knew Lucas would be willing to pay whatever the price if the information was deemed essential.

"Yes." Lucas simply couldn't understand how Victoria had gotten involved with this...or why the exchange would have turned deadly. There was no visible logic in play. That was why he'd sent Lucky. The one rule Jennifer had was that she never met face-to-face with anyone who could mark her as taking sides. She only delivered via totally neutral contacts.

"I'll keep trying to run down Lucky," Ian said, pushing to his feet, "Simon and Jim will keep us briefed on the situation there. If you have other con-tacts who might be of assistance, we could use what-ever we can get."

"That's the problem." Lucas lifted his gaze to Ian's. "None of my other contacts have anything on Keaton. Only Jennifer and now she's dead."

And Victoria and Lucky were missing.

With effort, Lucas stood. "I'm going to pay a visit to the brownstone." Keaton's office.

"That might not be a good idea," Ian countered. "If this is about Keaton, we may want to wait for his next step. Applying pressure might accelerate the situation."

Ian had a point but Lucas was not prepared to wait this out. Not with Victoria in danger and Lucky most likely in the same boat.

Slade Keaton had no idea onto whose toes he had just stepped.

If Victoria and Lucky were unharmed, the man might just survive his blunder.

Chapter Seven

12:15 p.m.

"What're you doing?" Lucky had struggled to regain her composure as Garrett had driven back and forth half a dozen times between the main highway and the rise overlooking the prison or institution or whatever it was.

If those people at the clinic had brought Victoria here, Mr. Camp and the others had to have a plan. Lucky wanted to be part of that plan.

This was her fault.

She should never have left that clinic.

Garrett turned into the drive of one of the houses at the end of the road nearest the main highway. "What're you doing now?" Some of the panic had subsided and Lucky felt more calm and rational. But frustration with Garrett's silence and his strange behavior was getting to her.

He didn't answer, just parked the truck and got out. She wrenched her door open and bounded out after him. "Really, Garrett, talk to me!" Why the heck had she let him put her off this long? She had to have suffered temporary insanity. Lucky might be new at the agency but she wasn't stupid. This was a serious, dangerous situation. She needed to know what was going on. "Maybe I should speak directly to Mr. Camp."

Garrett wheeled around and strode toward her. She stalled, abruptly knocked off her newly gained equilibrium by his lethal expression. She backed up a step as he stalked in toe-to-toe with her.

"Give me your cell."

That nonchalant tone he'd tossed around from the moment he'd burst into the building where Mr. Camp's contact had committed suicide had disappeared the moment he laid eyes on the place where those people had taken Mrs. Colby-Camp. But this deadly glare now focused on her was new.

She grabbed on to the disintegrating thread of her courage and shook her head firmly. "I told you I lost my cell phone."

Before she could fathom his intent he reached out and patted her down.

"Hey!" She tried to wiggle out of his reach. "You can't do that!"

He finished roving his hands over her body. "I just did." Then he executed a sharp turn and strode toward the house. He kept walking until he'd rounded the rear corner.

Fury obliterated the helpless feelings Lucky had endured all morning. She raced to the front of the house, up the steps and to the door. She banged hard on the door. "Is anyone there?" She banged more aggressively. "I need help!"

No answer. No barking dog. Not a sound.

"Please!" She banged some more. "Call the police!"

Expecting Garrett to come drag her away, she kept an eye out for him to reappear. He might have been sent by Mr. Camp but this was wrong. Her instincts were screaming at her. She pounded a couple more times.

Nothing.

Lucky turned around on the porch. The stillness of the landscape had that too familiar sinking feeling dragging down her fragile bravado. Dense woods edged up on either side of the long, deserted stretch. Only the few houses scattered along the last three or four miles broke the pattern of endless green.

They hadn't driven that far from the city. There had to be someone out here somewhere.

Reality invaded, making her mouth go dry.

It was the middle of the day on a weekday. People were likely at work. Was school still in session? If any kids were at home, would they call the police rather than answer the door? Lucky beat on the door again, her determination wilting faster than a week-old bouquet of roses.

Garrett hadn't come after her.

She surveyed the yard and road again. Her gaze tripped over his truck.

Had he taken the keys when he'd gotten out?

Before the thought had fully formed, she was down the steps and across the yard. She jerked the driver's door open and launched herself into the seat. Her fingers landed on the keys still in the ignition.

Victory sent a blast of adrenaline through her. She slid to the edge of the seat and stomped the clutch before turning the key. The truck rolled and she quickly pressed her right foot on the brake. A second twist of the key and the engine roared to life.

Lucky stared at the gear shifter on the floor. She'd driven a straight shift…once. Keeping the clutch pushed in, she moved the gearshift into what she hoped was Reverse. Then she slowly released the clutch and the brake simultaneously.

The truck jostled backward. Success sent her lips spreading wide. She twisted from the waist far enough to see behind her, so as to keep the truck out of the ditch. She nudged the accelerator….

Then the driver's door opened.

Lucky jumped. Her foot relaxed from the accelerator and the truck jerked once before the engine died.

The short black barrel of a gun leveled on her face. "Get out."

Fear clumped in her throat. If Garrett had intended to kill her he would have done so hours ago. He was supposed to be on the same team. Tightening her fingers on the steering wheel, she said, "No." She shoved in the clutch, reached for the key once more and gave it a twist.

A strong hand manacled her arm and hauled her out of the truck. Her foot slid off the clutch and the truck jerked again, the engine dying.

Garrett put her firmly aside and climbed into the truck. He started the engine.

A new kind of terror burst in her chest. Was he leaving her?

The truck moved forward until it had disappeared behind the house.

Fury chased away the new fear. Lucky wasn't taking any more grief from this man. She ran. She hit the pavement and kept running toward the main highway. Someone would come along. All she had to do was keep heading back toward the city.

If she could remember the way. She'd been pretty upset when they'd driven out here.

Wait. She mentally flipped through the vague memories of the past few minutes. The next house wasn't that far away. Maybe someone would be home there.

The echo of shoe soles slapping against pavement sounded behind her. She glanced back. Garrett was closing in. A blast of adrenaline had her legs moving faster. If he caught her before she reached the next house, she would never get away.

Why was she running? Confusion twisted inside her. He'd said Mr. Camp had sent him…but why wouldn't he tell her what was happening? He could be lying to her. How was she supposed to know? How had a simple errand for Mr. Camp and an even simpler task of accompanying Mrs. Colby-Camp to an appointment have gone so incredibly wrong so fast? Everything had spiraled out of control.

Lucky felt scared and confused. She wasn't prepared for this.

An arm banded around her waist, jerked her off her feet and swept her backward, as if underscoring her last thought. The sudden change in momentum put Garrett off balance and they tumbled to the ground on the side of the road. Though the impact knocked the breath out of Lucky, she struggled to get away. He fought to hold on to her. They rolled over the edge of the road's shoulder and down…down… down.

Tangled in waist-deep grass, they hit the bottom of the ditch. She grunted with the final impact of his body against hers. The world spun. How deep was this ditch? She tried to focus on the grass…where it disappeared above them, rising up to meet the road.

Garrett got up. He glared at her for a beat before lugging her up with him.

She'd had enough. Lucky launched back into action. She kicked him and punched him and yelled with all her might.

He tried to hold her, but she twisted in his grip. They toppled to the ground again.

This time he flattened her against the grass with his body weight. "That's enough!"

She glared at him. "Let me go or I will start screaming again."

"You scream and I will shut you up."

He wasn't kidding. The rage flaring in his eyes, stiffening in his body, was undeniable.

Lucky lost it.

She screamed at the top of her lungs.

His hand closed over her mouth. "My orders are to protect you."

She tried to argue. To inform him that *this* did not feel like protection. But his hand remained firmly in place over her mouth.

"Your boss is in that place," he growled, his palm still muffling her protests. "Do you want to help her or not?"

Lucky couldn't breathe. Her heart was pounding too hard to inhale through her nose. She managed only a nod.

"Then you have to listen to me." He dragged in a jagged breath of his own. "You don't know this place. I do. You have to believe me when I say that this is bad. This is real bad. Our next move will very likely determine if your boss survives or not."

Dear God. Lucky's determination wilted with resignation. Could she possibly trust this man?

He claimed Mr. Camp had sent him, and he hadn't killed her...yet. The very idea that she was alive and all those other people were dead had to tilt things in

his favor. She studied his eyes, tried to read something beyond the frustration and impatience. She had
to trust him.

She had no other choice.

Lucky nodded her agreement to listen to him. The
pressure on her mouth eased. Despite her brand-new
promise she had to fight the instinct to scream.

Garrett braced his hands on the ground on either
side of her and pushed to his feet, lifting his body
easily from hers.

She scrambled on all fours to put a few feet between them and got up. "What kind of place is it?"

He dusted off his trousers. "I'll explain everything
later. Right now we have to get back to the house."
He exhaled, tried to expel some of the frustration. "I
have to figure this out."

Before she could ask what house, he climbed the
bank opposite the road and started into the woods.

Lucky pushed the hair out of her face and followed
the path he'd taken. It wasn't easy to wade through
the underbrush that she wasn't quite tall enough to
march over as he had. When she caught up to him,
she asked, "What house are you talking about?"

"This one." He broke the tree line, entering a
grassy yard.

She stared at the back of the pale yellow house
and realized it was the one she'd just run from. "Do
you know who lives here?" She hustled to catch up
to him again. "Is that why you stopped here?" That
would be convenient but also highly unlikely.

He didn't stop until he'd reached the back porch. At the door, he opened the screen and elbowed one of the panes of glass in the upper part of the door. The glass shattered. He cleared the jagged pieces from the mullion and reached inside. Three seconds later he opened the door and walked into the house. The wooden screen door slammed shut behind him.

Lucky stood there, looking from the broken glass on the wood floor of the porch to the dark interior of the house where he'd disappeared.

When she'd pulled herself together, she opened the screen door and gingerly stepped over the broken glass. As soon as she'd located Garrett, she demanded, "Are you insane?"

He didn't respond but he shot her a look that let her know he didn't appreciate her remark. It didn't matter that he hadn't turned on a light inside the house. The meager light that filtered in through the partially closed blinds allowed her to see the feral look on his face.

Without a word he gave her his back and resumed his trek through the apparently deserted house.

Lucky took a minute to get her bearings. There was furniture in the house, framed photographs on the wall. People lived here. There had to be a phone.

Conscious of his movements, she eased into the nearest room. It was a bedroom and had no phone. She silently moved back into the hall, then into two more bedrooms without phones. What was wrong with these people? Didn't they know that there should be a phone in every room of the house?

She found none in the living room either.

Fear and dread tied her stomach into knots once more.

She went back to the kitchen. Where was Garrett?

Biting her lower lip, she moved quickly around the kitchen.

There.

A phone hung on the wall next to the refrigerator. Relief melted her knees. She hurried across the room. It was the old-fashioned kind, with a long, curly cord. Lucky didn't care as long as it worked.

She eased the receiver from its hook. The dial tone was like music to her ears. Holding her breath, she began entering the number for the agency. If Mr. Camp sent Garrett he shouldn't mind her confirming his story.

A broad hand clamped down on the face of the phone, depressing the hook, before tearing the old-fashioned instrument completely off the wall.

"No calls," he growled. The fierce expression that still claimed his face now extended to his voice, making the growl animal-like.

Lucky dropped the receiver and it clattered on the floor. "Why can't I call the office?" Fear trickled into her veins.

"Stop asking questions. I don't have any answers for you yet." He grabbed her by the arm and hauled her into the hallway of the ranch-style home.

When he reached the largest of the three bedrooms he flung her to the bed. A new kind of fear awakened inside her.

"Don't move," he warned before turning away.

She exhaled a shaky breath, immediately exiling thoughts of physical assault from her brain. He just wanted her where he could keep an eye on her. As she watched he rifled through the closet. Eventually he pulled out a pair of jeans and tossed them on the bed next to her. While she watched, he emptied his pockets onto the dresser and placed his cell phone and gun there as well. He toed off the loafers he wore and reached for the fly of his trousers.

Lucky turned away.

The whir of the zipper was followed by the whisper of fabric against skin. In her peripheral vision she saw the trousers he'd been wearing land on the floor before he tugged on the pair of jeans and fastened them. When she heard the zipper go up, she turned toward him as he poked first one foot and then the other into his shoes.

"Just tell me," she said calmly, which amazed her, "what is it we're going to do?" If they couldn't call anyone, surely he had a plan.

As if she hadn't said a word, he stalked back to the closet and started prowling once more. The jeans were a size too small judging by the way they looked shrink-wrapped to his backside and thighs. She blinked and focused her attention on the dresser.

He'd left the gun lying there.

Anticipation made her nerves jump. She visually measured the distance between him and the dresser and her position on the bed and the dresser. About equal. If he was distracted enough, she might make it. Having the gun and the upper hand would be nice for a change.

As if he'd heard her thoughts, he turned around and strode back to the dresser. He filled the tight pockets of the jeans with the change and whatnot and tucked the gun into his waistband.

He grabbed her by the arm and hauled her out of the room. After checking the closet in a second bedroom and finding girl clothes, he moved to the third. This one was a boy's room. A teenager, considering the clothes in the closet. Garrett picked out a black rock band T-shirt and proceeded to unbutton his grass-stained white shirt.

Lucky lapsed into a barrage of possibilities. Maybe someone in the family would come home and then they'd have to call the office since the homeowners would no doubt call the police. A twinge of pain accompanied the thought that nothing she or anyone else did now would help the driver or that lady Jennifer.

Garrett peeled off his shirt and Lucky's attention riveted to his back.

She swallowed hard. Scars. Lots of scars. The kind one gets when physically tortured. He turned around to face her as he pushed his arms into the sleeves. There were not so many scars on his chest, just lots of defined muscle. She'd never seen a six-pack like that. Not in real life anyway.

When he'd dragged the tee down his torso, he threaded his fingers through his hair. "You hungry?"

He wouldn't have startled her more if he'd asked her to remove her own clothes. "Seriously?" He had to be joking. She still had the dead woman's blood on her clothes, her boss had been kidnapped and *he* refused her even one phone call. Even criminals got one phone call.

Without further explanation, he grabbed her again and hauled her into the kitchen.

"I can walk without your assistance," she grumbled. It wasn't necessary for him to lug her around like a rag doll.

He didn't spare her a look, much less a comment since to do so would have interfered with his rummaging through the refrigerator. Lucky studied the broken phone, bemoaning the fact that there was no way to repair it.

He withdrew a couple of canned sodas, some sandwich meats and mayo. After setting those items aside, he walked to the sink and washed his hands. Lucky felt like she was in a low-budget movie where not even the stars would survive the impending face-off with the monster. A monster they couldn't quite see but whose devastation had already left a broad path.

A half-eaten loaf of bread sat on the counter. He

opened it, sniffed, then removed four slices. He did the same with the meats, ensuring they were still edible. Hunger pangs attacked her determination. She was hungry. But it just didn't feel like the right thing to do under the circumstances.

The pop of the soda tab sent her over the edge. She had to eat. Or at least drink something.

At the sink she scrubbed her hands again until her skin felt as if it would peel right off the bone. Then she moved to the counter where he'd laid out all the fixings and reached for the bread, careful not to allow her arm to brush against him. When she'd completed her sandwich, he placed a soda on the counter.

"Thank you." She didn't look at him. At this point she had basically bottomed out mentally. Anything she said would be the wrong thing.

He'd inhaled two sandwiches before she'd nibbled away half of hers. He stared out the kitchen window at the woods that bordered the yard. She wanted to ask him what was next. They had to do something soon. Someone had to be doing something. She needed to know, to understand what was happening.

As if her mind simply had to lock on to something, she kept replaying the look in his eyes when she'd asked him if he was insane. She'd hit a nerve. Had someone in his family been mentally unstable? Had he suffered some sort of trauma because of it? Or was he the unstable one? That couldn't be right. Lucas wouldn't send a crazy man to back her up. Unless he hadn't. Lucky just didn't know about him yet, but she knew more than she wanted to about crazy people. Her mother was way, way on the other side of normal.

Lucky pushed away the troubling memories of her mother and focused on the here and now. The reasons for kidnapping Mrs. Colby-Camp were likely the standard fare. Money, revenge. But why bring her to that foreboding, prisonlike place just down the road? If that place Garrett had called hell was a mental institution, wouldn't that mean numerous staff members would have to be involved with the kidnapping?

Maybe not. If Mrs. Colby-Camp's identity was not revealed, she could just be another incoming patient. Now that Lucky thought about it, a place like that would be a handy way to hold a person hostage.

Garrett turned from the window. Lucky put aside the worrisome theories.

"I have to make some calls," he said. That he didn't look at her as he spoke escalated the worry already crushing in on her. "Once I have the details I need, I'll formulate a strategy for the next move."

"We aren't going to call the agency? Won't Mr. Camp need a status?" She bit the inside of her jaw. Seemed like the only right strategy. What was his motive for avoiding that step?

His gaze locked on hers. "That would be a mistake at this point."

Lucky shook her head, the sandwich turning to

rock in her stomach. "Why would that be a mistake? If you work for Mr. Camp—"

"Trust me," he said as he pushed away from the counter, "even he can't help your boss now."

Chapter Eight

Dakota stepped out the back door and into the yard. He needed some air. Lucky Malone hadn't demanded any additional answers and Dakota was grateful. He almost laughed. Imagine, him grateful for that small concession.

It was this place.

He braced his hands on his hips and closed his eyes.

A cold sweat formed on his skin.

He'd put the past and this place so far behind him that it wasn't until he'd topped that hill that he'd fully recognized where he was.

How the hell had he ended up here?

Returning to Chicago as Dakota Garrett had been a major coup for him. The past no longer ruled him. He had beaten it. It would never haunt him again, never own him again.

His jaw hardened against the doubt that attempted to slither up his spine. He would not feel that again.

Ever.

His cell vibrated. He pulled it from his pocket.

His hand shook, detonating a charge of fury in his gut. Tightening his grip until the phone case nearly cracked, he checked the screen. It was Keaton.

Every instinct stirring inside Dakota warned that this was somehow Keaton's fault. Couldn't be coincidence.

He would soon know. "Garrett."

"The local authorities have responded to the scene where the driver was killed."

Dakota had figured as much. "And the Colby Agency?"

"They've been notified. Two members are on the scene now."

"My kills were clean," Dakota assured his boss. "I had no other option."

"Not to worry. A witness has come forward."

Dakota stilled. "You don't say?" He'd doubted that anyone who might be loitering in that neighborhood would come forward for the police unless they were a victim in some way and maybe not even then.

"A bag lady who spends her nights in the building directly across the street," Keaton went on. "She confirmed that the two armed victims killed the driver and attempted to fire on the hero who came out of nowhere to save the pretty lady trapped inside that old building." Keaton made a sound that might have been his version of a chuckle. "Those are her exact words."

"I've been called worse," Dakota retorted with his

own jab at humor he didn't feel. There was nothing amusing about the situation from his perspective.

"So you're in the clear on that one, but…"

He'd known a but was coming.

"The woman gave a fair description of your vehicle. Blue, two-door, older model truck. She even managed to recall the first three numbers of your license plate."

Not good, but not the end of the world. Dakota wasn't worried. He was a licensed investigator and he had a permit to carry a weapon. He didn't want any part of this official investigation or any other, but he had no call to be concerned. "If they run me down," he offered, "I'll deal with that then."

"Agreed. More imperative at the moment," Keaton went on, "have you arrived at any workable scenarios for rescuing Victoria?"

Who was this Victoria that she appeared so damned important to the head of the Equalizers? "The only scenario I've arrived at has nothing to do with a rescue." Dakota didn't mince words. He wanted Keaton to know he was not happy about this.

"What does that mean, Garrett?"

The hint of warning in the man's tone didn't put Dakota off in the least. "It means—" he glanced at Malone who watched him from the kitchen window "—that I'm close to the location of her cell phone, as you likely know." It wasn't like he couldn't view the results of the search. "The location doesn't work for me." Something else the boss also no doubt knew.

Tense silence hung in the air between them for two beats. Dakota's body stiffened with the mounting anticipation.

"You're familiar with the location?"

Fury boiled up inside Dakota again before he could stop it. "Byrd Institute." The name left a bitter taste in his mouth. "Oh, yeah. I know the place."

The silence emanating from Keaton was broken only by the soft but distinct click of computer keys. He was running a search on the name. Uncertainty nudged Dakota. Maybe Keaton didn't know about the place. Maybe he hadn't set up this whole screwed-up scenario.

"The sanitarium?" Keaton asked, something like surprise in his voice.

"That's the place." Dakota threaded his fingers through his hair. The urge to get the hell out of here was almost overwhelming. He shoved the inkling of fear aside. He hadn't felt that particular emotion in years.

"You're certain?"

"Unless the GPS made a mistake," Dakota snapped. "And I doubt that's the case." What was with this guy? The Colby Agency could deal with this. Dakota should drop Malone off at the nearest convenience store and let her call in. This wasn't his problem. He couldn't figure out why it would be

Keaton's. And Dakota still wasn't convinced that his boss hadn't somehow set this up.

As for the GPS system they used, it was state-of-the-art even if it wasn't legal. Tracking cell phones required a warrant inducing the carrier's cooperation. The cell phone belonging to Victoria Colby-Camp had definitely entered the Byrd facility. It had now fallen off the grid which meant the phone had been shut off and the battery removed. Not even the carrier would be able to track it now beyond the last cell tower it passed.

"I'm pulling up the floor plans of the sanitarium now," Keaton said, the sound of his hands moving efficiently across the computer keys underscoring his words. "I'll download them to your phone."

"Why?"

That was a question few would have dared ask a boss like Keaton. But this was different on a level no one else could possibly comprehend. To understand Dakota's position would be to know the darkest, most painful details of his past. No one knew those. No one. Whatever Keaton's motive here, he couldn't know the specific details.

That file had been closed when Dakota was seventeen, right after his mother's death.

He had every intention of keeping it that way.

"It's imperative that you determine who is behind this abduction."

Dakota shook his head, didn't care that the man couldn't see the response. "I think you need a different man for the job." He wouldn't do this. And he damned sure didn't intend to explain his reasons. Keaton's silence had Dakota pacing in the ankle-deep grass. But the pacing wasn't related to any intimidation Keaton might attempt. It was about the past— memories he didn't want to experience again.

"Your personal knowledge of the facility would be invaluable. Based on my findings there are several staff members, including the administrator, with whom you are familiar who still work there."

Dakota froze. There was no way Keaton could have access to that file. No way in hell. It didn't exist anymore—at least not the original. Dakota had destroyed it. Copies shouldn't have existed. Why would Keaton have looked for a file which, for all intents and purposes, didn't exist? And why hadn't he brought this matter up before now? Whatever he thought he knew, Dakota wasn't that person anymore…not in mind or in name.

"Like I said," Dakota repeated, "you'll need someone else for this one."

One, two, three seconds elapsed, then four and five. "I need you for this one. Keep Malone away from the Colby Agency and get me the name and the motive behind this abduction. But, above all else, get Victoria safely out of there."

Keaton ended the call before Dakota could argue. He stared at the screen a long moment before shoving it into the pocket of his borrowed jeans.

No way.

He scanned the tree line and drew in a deep, steadying breath. No way in hell. He closed his eyes and shook his head as if those simple gestures would somehow make this nightmare go away.

"Well?"

Dakota opened his eyes. Malone had stepped out the back door. She stood on the porch, her arms crossed over her chest. "What?" he demanded. He should never have taken her anywhere. He shouldn't have gotten involved, direct order or not. If he'd ever met a woman more innocent, more in need of a savior, he had no recall of the encounter. And he was no savior...not even for a woman who stirred those long dead warrior instincts of his.

"I think I should call my agency. I need—"

"Your agency is already on the case. The police are investigating the scene now. Two of your colleagues are on site. You don't need to be concerned."

"That means they'll be coming soon," she said hopefully.

He walked toward her. "They're developing their strategy." It wasn't exactly a lie. Common sense dictated the steps to be taken.

"How much longer are we staying here?" She reached up and tucked her hair behind her ears, visibly growing more nervous as he neared. "I mean, the owners will show up at some point. Shouldn't we get moving?"

His fingers itched to know if her hair felt as silky as it looked. He should just let her go. It would be better for her and for him. To hell with Keaton. "They won't be back for three more days."

She frowned. "How do you know?" She gestured toward the kitchen behind her. "There's milk in the fridge. Bread on the counter."

"The mailbox."

Her frown deepened with confusion.

"These rural routes have substitute carriers as often as not. They keep a note on the inside of the mailbox door reminding whoever happens to be delivering on any given day of the residents at the address. Whenever someone has their mail held for a few days or whatever, the regular carrier notes it in that same place so no one forgets and leaves the mail."

There were all sorts of ways to determine when people were on vacation versus just away for the day. Like the fact that they clearly had dogs, evidenced by the food and water bowls, but there was no sign of dogs in the house or yard. But the most telling of all was that the shutoff valves to the kitchen and bathroom sinks as well as the toilet were in the off position. Turning them off prevented flooding in the event a leak started when the family was away. He'd had to turn the water on in both the kitchen and the hall bath.

"If the police and my agency are working the case," she ventured, taking another approach, "why are we hiding out like this? I don't understand why Mr. Camp would insist we continue to lay low." The suspicion that flickered in her eyes was unmistakable.

Dakota couldn't answer her question. Primarily because he didn't want to come up with another lie. As nuts as it sounded, lying to her felt wrong. He didn't like this and he was sick of the game Keaton had decided to play. However he had gotten his hands on a copy Dakota's file—a copy that wasn't supposed to exist—there had to be a motive behind the move that Dakota wasn't going to like. Regardless of Slade Keaton's interest in the Colby Agency and Victoria Colby-Camp, Dakota wanted no part of it. As for Lucky Malone, he suspected that she just happened to be at the wrong place at the wrong time.

He held his palms upward. "I can't answer any of those questions for you." He turned his back and strode back into the middle of the yard. He needed to think without her hounding him. Without having to look into those big, hopeful eyes.

Malone moved up behind him, obviously not ready to give up.

"Don't ask me any more questions I can't answer," he said before she could speak again. He didn't want to talk about this. Dakota had gone to great lengths to ensure he couldn't be traced to that name…to that life. Somehow Keaton had figured it out. And after he had, why had he hired Dakota? Employers didn't typically hire applicants with a history of hard-core mental illness.

There could only be one reason. Keaton had an agenda.

Damn him.

"I know you can answer this one," Malone said as she moved closer still.

His body tensed in reaction to her nearness. To the sound of her voice. What the hell was wrong with him? He should just drop her off somewhere and then he should disappear. Why not? He'd done it before. But his entire being rebelled against the idea. Another path he had no desire to travel a second time.

He'd thought that part of his life was behind him. For good.

"What is it about that place we saw that makes you so nervous?" She glanced in the direction of the institute. "What kind of place is it?"

He laughed; it sounded pained and rusty even to him. "I'm not afraid of anything, lady." He wasn't. Not now. Maybe he hadn't even been afraid then. Dakota swallowed back the denial that attempted to climb into his throat. Why the hell was he even talking to her about this?

"When you saw that place," she pressed, "your face changed. I saw the terror in your eyes. There's something you're not telling me."

There was a whole hell of a lot he wasn't telling her. "What's this? Amateur psychology hour?" He clenched his jaw to restrain any outward expression of the anxiety building inside him. Damn it.

"You said the place is hell," she challenged, throwing his words back at him. "How do you know?"

His cell vibrated. Dakota gritted his teeth. He stared at the display screen for two more rings. He shouldn't answer Keaton this time. He'd been the one to end the last call. But the truth was, even if Dakota didn't want to acknowledge it, if an innocent victim had been transported into that facility—whoever she might be—she was in for a nightmare she couldn't begin to comprehend. Could he really just walk away and pretend he didn't know?

He accepted the call. "Garrett."

"I understand this is difficult," Keaton admitted, his tone weary or reluctant, "but you know what happens behind those walls. You can't walk away from this. Not and let them do to her what they did to you."

More of that unbridled fury tightened Dakota's lips at the idea that his boss had just read his mind. This guy had no idea what he was asking. Dakota stepped away from Malone and muttered, "How did you get my file?" Years after he'd left Chicago far behind, he'd returned once. His mission had been simple— break into the hall of records at Juvie and take his file. He'd burned every single page. No matter that it had been sealed, he hadn't wanted to take any chances.

"Your case worker kept a copy of the file."

Impossible. That was a breach of security, not to mention an ethics infraction. "She must be retired or dead by now." Uncertainty niggled at him. Rules were broken all the time. He had broken more than his share.

"She is. But she left behind a very cooperative husband who likes nothing better than bragging about all the cases where his lovely wife helped out a troubled teen. Particularly the very difficult ones."

Every vein in Dakota's body throbbed with a volatile mixture of emotions. Rage, regret, pain...too many to name.

A man like Keaton wouldn't stop with the usual background research. He would want to know everything. Just because no one else had been able to dig up that ugly past didn't mean he wouldn't be able to. Dakota should have recognized that about the man at the initial interview. He should have seen this coming.

"Why did you hire me?" Dakota hated that his voice sounded weak. He wasn't weak, not anymore.

"Because I knew a man who'd been as deep into hell as you would prove more useful and resourceful than a dozen of the most highly skilled and experienced others who lined up for the three positions I had to offer."

Dakota knew the explanation wasn't meant as a compliment. It was fact. Keaton operated on fact alone. Dakota doubted a man more emotionless than Keaton existed. He had recognized an asset and he'd seized it.

"You know the goal and the obstacles," Keaton said, getting down to business. "The question is, are you willing to accept the assignment?"

Dakota glanced at Malone who waited only two or three yards away, her eyes filled with worry and frustration.

She wasn't his problem. This Victoria wasn't his problem. What made either of them relevant to Keaton?

"Quid pro quo, Keaton," Dakota announced, the inspiration only just coming to him. "You know my deepest, darkest secret, so tell me one of yours. If you impress me, I'll take the job. If you don't, it's *adios, amigo.*"

Silence expanded between them.

Dakota had him there. He mentally counted off the seconds. Four, five, six. Just to see how long Keaton would hold out. Nine, ten.

"She is key to my learning certain things about my past." There was another extended silence. "I need that information."

Of all the myriad possibilities Dakota had considered in those few seconds, this was assuredly not one of them. Was this part of why Slade Keaton was so secretive? Dakota could definitely relate despite having no desire to.

"If she dies," he ventured, "your opportunity to find the truth may die with her?"

"Yes."

Dakota scrubbed his free hand over his mouth.

Fourteen years. It had taken him fourteen long years to put this place behind him. Only last year had he mustered up the courage to return to Chicago—the home that had never really been home to him. He'd made a decision that he would make it home, that he would never allow anything to keep him away again. It was the final proof of his triumph. It was a test to prove he could do it.

He had a new life now. A new name. The past was way behind him. They couldn't touch him anymore.

Unless he chose to let them.

His cheek pulsed with the tension of his hard-set jaw. Dakota had spent a lifetime running away from exactly what Keaton was running toward. Dakota understood all too well that driving need to find the nirvana that would somehow set a man free.

Keaton broke into his thoughts. "You can get inside more quickly than anyone else without revealing your true agenda."

Dakota was intimately familiar with the institute's security. No one got in without an invitation from the director. Dr. Lionel Byrd. The images of white coats and moans of pain that accompanied the name made Dakota's gut seize.

"You know that once I get in, they'll never let me out alive." He knew too much. Remembered the things they wanted certain patients to forget. That he'd escaped and was never found was the one black mark on that freak Byrd's otherwise perfect record.

He wouldn't allow the same mistake twice.

The first few years after Dakota had escaped, he'd sworn that one day he would go back. He'd go back and he'd kill that madman. Put a stop to his evil endeavors.

But Dakota had never taken that step. He'd pretended to forget the whole idea. He could deny it all day long, but fear, pure and simple, had kept him clear of the Byrd Institute. Until now he hadn't so much as dared to think the name, except in the occasional nightmare.

"I will see that you are released," Keaton guaranteed. "You have my word."

For the first time since he'd taken the position with the Equalizers, Dakota wondered if there was any way under the sun he could trust this man.

Malone had moved in front of him. She studied Dakota's face, searched his eyes in hopes of learning something about the conversation.

"Garrett," Keaton urged, "don't fail me and I will not fail you."

Dakota laughed. He had been thirteen years old the last time he'd believed in anyone besides himself. Despite that glaring fact, he said, "Consider it done."

Keaton wanted to know the details of his entry strategy. Dakota couldn't give him any meticulously calculated steps.

There was just one that mattered.

And the timing had to be perfect for it to work.

Chapter Nine

2:00 p.m.

Chicago P.D.'s contact, Sean Ames, waited patiently while Lucas moved carefully around the crime scene. The bodies had been removed but the markers placed by the forensics techs remained in place. Ian had convinced Lucas not to confront Keaton until they had more to go on. Struggling to keep his emotions from overwhelming his logic, he had agreed to ignore his strongest instinct and delay that move.

Now, as he stood here, surrounded by the evidence of senseless death, he wasn't so sure he'd made the right decision. There was nothing that gave so much as a hint as to why this shoot-out had gone down. The two male victims had been identified. Mercenaries for hire, their allegiance to the dollar and not the employer. Simon was running down background info on the two. The witness who had come forward insisted that the man who'd killed the two mercenaries had been a hero. That he'd saved the young woman, who, based on her description, was Malone. The witness had seen no one else. Nicole Reed-Michaels, Ian's wife and a Colby investigator herself, was following up with the witness.

Where had Victoria been during the shoot-out? Jim and Ian were attempting to nail down a location on Victoria's cell phone. As soon as Chicago P.D.'s lab confirmed that the blood at the scene matched the victims, with none unaccounted for, Lucas would be able to breathe again.

He studied the place where Jennifer had fallen and shook his head. He would find who did this.

"Lucas."

He turned to Ames and raised his eyebrows in question.

"I was able to get the M.E. to do a preliminary review of the bodies, per your request."

"I appreciate that, Ames." Lucas needed all the details he could gather as quickly as possible. Having good contacts with the local authorities was immensely useful to that end.

Ames acknowledged the thanks with a nod. "The M.E.'s preliminary conclusion on the female vic is that the fatal gunshot was self-inflicted."

A wave of disbelief crashed into Lucas. "He's certain?" That conclusion was even more confusing than the rest of this strewn puzzle.

Ames gave a succinct nod. "He wouldn't say one way or the other unless he was damned certain. The lab confirmed that all the blood—" he gestured to the ground "—belonged to the four victims."

Relief flooded Lucas's chest. "Thank you, Sean." Lucas used the man's first name as further indication of how much he appreciated his help. "I've seen enough."

Ames made conversation about the rise in random crimes as he secured the scene and then walked with Lucas to where they had parked their cars on the opposite side of the street. Before driving away he assured Lucas that he would keep him apprised of every step of their investigation. An APB had been issued for both Victoria and Lucky.

Tow trucks had arrived to transport the vehicles involved to the Chicago P.D. crime lab for further analysis. Lucky's purse had been left inside the car. Where the hell was she? Where was Victoria? Lucas sat in his car for long minutes, watching the removal of the vehicles. He banished the fear roaring beneath his skin and summoned the part of himself that he had retired six months ago—the ruthless, relentless intelligence agent and master spy who never failed to accomplish his mission. There was no room for emotion now. And no time for second guessing. Action, swift and decisive, was essential.

He opened his cell phone and put through a call to Ian Michaels. "There's nothing else to be gained here." He passed along the lab results as well as the M.E.'s conclusion. Ian had no news from Nicole. "Notify me the instant you have an update," Lucas said as he settled his gaze on the run-down building where his longtime friend had lost her life. "I'll keep trying to get in touch with my contact who can track Victoria's cell since it wasn't found at the scene."

"Are you returning to the office?"

Lucas's lips tightened, then he said, "No. I'm going to the brownstone."

This time Ian didn't argue.

Keaton was the only lead Lucas had and even that one was nothing more than gut instinct.

Lucas's instincts had brought down far larger and more dangerous prey than Slade Keaton.

Whatever Keaton's game, it was over.

Chapter Ten

5:05 p.m.

Lucky had waited long enough for answers. Garrett had spent the past few hours alternately speaking to someone on his cell and studying its screen. He'd ignored her every question, putting her off each time she attempted to interrupt. She wasn't going to stand for this a minute more.

She stalked across the kitchen, arms folded over her chest, and stared up at him. He was tall, even leaning against the counter the way he was. She disregarded the hint of uncertainty that whispered through her veins. He made her feel even more vulnerable, needy—the kind of need that only a woman understood. No man, certainly not a stranger, had ever succeeded in making her feel that way. "What's happening? We've been here for hours and you've told me nothing."

Several seconds elapsed before he looked up from his phone. When he did, her breath hitched. He frowned. "I'll brief you on the details you need to know when it's time." He shifted his attention back to the screen of his high-tech smart phone.

Outrage rumbled inside her, vaporizing those silly, softer feelings. Okay. Lucky had been patient long enough. She was fed up with being treated as though she was not as deeply involved in this as her self-professed savior was.

"I'm only a personal assistant," she snapped, another shot of anger blasting through her, "and I'm new to the agency, but I'm not a child or an idiot. If whatever you're planning has anything to do with my boss or me, I am a part of it. So start talking, Mr. Garrett."

He leveled his gaze on hers, his brown eyes assessing her long enough to undermine her bravado. "What do you want to know? Specifically."

She blinked. "Why are we still waiting here? Why aren't we doing something?" That was a good start.

He placed his cell on the counter and folded his arms over his broad chest. She didn't know if he was matching her body language or mocking it and that annoyed the heck out of her. What frustrated her even more was that she couldn't help but notice the width of his shoulders. Or how he smelled like sweet fresh air. She'd definitely lost it.

Then he leaned toward her and placed his hands on the counter, one hand on either side of her. "We can't move for several hours yet—"

"Hours?" She held her breath to prevent inhaling

more of that appealing scent of his. This close she couldn't help studying every lean detail of his face. Focus, Lucky! He'd said hours. Was he out of his mind? Surely Mr. Camp wasn't in agreement with this plan. Mrs. Colby-Camp had been taken hours ago—far too many hours ago. Before she could calm herself Lucky said as much.

Garrett cocked his head, stared at her lips a moment then gave her a curious look. "Do you want answers or not?"

Exasperation replaced the burst of anger. "Keep going." She trembled inside as much from being trapped by his body as from her frustration…maybe more.

"We'll go in after your boss, but the timing is crucial. The strategy won't work unless the timing is perfect."

That still didn't explain anything. "Has Mr. Camp initiated any other strategies? Why aren't the police here?" People had been murdered by the criminals involved in Mrs. Colby-Camp's abduction! The Colby Agency would never disregard the law. That doubt she'd suffered several times already surfaced again. Had Mr. Camp really sent this man to watch over her? There were moments, like now, that his story just didn't feel right. And yet she couldn't stop wanting to fall into his arms and to allow him to assuage this unfamiliar restlessness stirring so deep inside her that she felt as if she might erupt into a volcano of heat.

"The people we're dealing with don't respond well to the police," Garrett said. The features of his face tightened visibly as he spoke. "If backed into a corner, they'll cut their losses and your boss will be the one to lose." The utter certainty in his eyes made her breath catch. "Trust me. In three decades they've never been caught. They never leave any evidence. They have disposal and cleanup down to a science."

Lucky flinched. "You're saying they would…" She licked her lips, wishing her throat wasn't so dry. "They would hurt her? Get rid of her?"

He nodded. "In a heartbeat."

"How do we know they haven't already hurt her?" A surge of fear forced her heart into a faster rhythm.

"We don't."

That wasn't the answer she'd wanted to hear, though she fully understood he was most likely right. She cleared the anxiety from her throat. "So when the time comes, what are we going to do?" She held her breath, tried to slow her pounding heart. Tried not to watch his mouth in anticipation of his lips moving.

"We're going in." He straightened, moved away from her and picked up his phone. He checked the screen, then slid the phone into the pocket of his jeans. As if their discussion was over, he strode to the refrigerator and looked inside.

She blinked away the image of his backside, cleared the lump of apprehension and need clogging her throat and resumed her interrogation. "Explain 'going in.'"

He turned around, a couple of slices of cheese in his hand, and bumped the refrigerator door shut with his hip. "We're arranging for a badge that identifies you as an employee of the institute. You'll go in and search for your boss while I create a distraction."

A new kind of fear clutched at her chest. "Even with a badge, are they just going to let me wander the halls of the place?" From the way he'd described the institute so far she couldn't imagine that being the case.

He shrugged, drawing her attention to the appealing way the T-shirt molded to his body. He looked strong. She should find that comforting but somehow she didn't. It was...distracting. Just as these crazy things he made her feel were.

"You'll need to be creative and careful," he advised. "I can get us inside and distract the powers that be, but the search and avoiding the wrong kind of attention are entirely up to you."

Lucky had no undercover operative training, no investigative training whatsoever. She was a terrible liar. She'd only fired a weapon once in her life and that hadn't ended well. Putting Mrs. Colby-Camp's well-being in Lucky's hands was a stunningly poor choice in strategy. Garrett couldn't be serious. The entire plan was risky and ridiculous. If Lucky was caught, would Mrs. Colby-Camp pay the price? Where was their backup or on-site support of any kind? This was not the way the Colby Agency carried out operations. Lucky might be new but she'd done her research before applying.

A cold, hard reality slammed into her churning thoughts.

Her eyes widened as the air rushed out of her lungs. "Mr. Camp didn't send you." It wasn't a question. Lucky suddenly understood that terrifying truth with absolute certainty.

DAKOTA MULLED OVER the best way to answer.

That he was even hesitating to simply toss out another automatic lie was unexpected. That this naive, clearly inexperienced woman could have sexual tension building in him was downright baffling. He stuck with the more experienced types. The ones who wanted or expected nothing more than physical release. This was way outside his comfort zone.

"There's no basis for your accusation." The statement seemed to puzzle her almost as much as his hesitation baffled him. He never hesitated. Some amount of collateral damage was unavoidable in most operations. That this woman was an innocent bystander wasn't his problem. "Why else would I have stopped those shooters from taking you out?" He held out his hands palms up in an open, why-would-I-lie gesture.

Her head moved from side to side, her gray eyes narrowing with mounting suspicion. "Mr. Camp and the Colby Agency would not take these kinds of risks. He and others from the agency would be here, preparing for this rescue. Mrs. Colby-Camp's life wouldn't be left hanging in the balance like this." She sucked in a breath as if she'd only just then been able to breathe. The uncertainty he'd seen in her eyes moments ago had transformed into slowly solidifying determination.

He might as well give her the facts. "Let me explain exactly what we're up against."

That determination in her eyes amped up a notch and she hiked up her chin in preparation for challenging whatever he offered next. He hadn't antipated this kind of resistance. Apparently he'd overestimated her naiveté. He'd damned sure underestimated her ability to distract him on a physical level.

"This place…" His throat tightened like a vise in spite of his resolve not to be affected. "This place has impenetrable security. Visitors are meticulously screened. Visitation is allowed only once per week and the activities of those visitors are limited to one confined area on the first floor. The registered patients are kept in private rooms on the top three floors." Images from the underground level invaded despite his resolve to keep them at bay. "Worst-case scenario she won't be with the registered patients."

Confusion claimed Malone's face, infused those big gray eyes with fear. "How can you know any of this?"

"She could be in Research." He banished the sounds from the past that murmured in his brain.

"Access is restricted to a handful of personnel. Getting in there will be impossible for you."

"Why would she be there? What's Research?"

"Depends upon the motive for her abduction. Money?" He shook his head. "Probably not. Revenge or leverage is the most likely scenario. Your boss either has something they want or she's crossed the wrong man."

Dr. Lionel Byrd.

Dakota's jaw clenched with hatred. The man would go to any lengths to accomplish his goal and he owned far too many others in positions of power to ever be stopped. He was the kind of man who could be stopped only one way—with a bullet between the eyes. If Dakota hadn't been such a coward, he would have taken care of that all those years ago. But he'd had only one thing on his mind: escape.

"How can we possibly hope to get her out?" Terror weighted Malone's voice.

Her fear made him want to protect her, the way he had never been protected. Maybe it was her painful past, but something about her drew him in on a level no one else had ever touched. He looked away from her, glanced at the clock above the refrigerator. They had less than six hours. Getting Malone fully prepared was essential. That had to be his focus. "We need to fuel up. There might not be another opportunity. Being sharp is essential." Maybe he could shift her attention with a sandwich. Or was it his attention that needed tweaking?

She shook her head. "I don't want anything. You have to tell me how this can possibly work."

He pushed away from the counter and moved back to the refrigerator. "Eat anyway. We need every advantage we can get." At this point they had only one—his intimate knowledge of the place and its operations.

"What do they do there?"

He'd expected she'd get around to that question eventually. Dakota sat the deli-style turkey slices and cheese on the counter. "It's a mental hospital." His teeth ground with the bitter taste that accompanied the words. Mayo. Needed that, too. He grabbed the jar, closed the door and reached for the sliced bread on the counter. "They treat patients, as far as the outside world knows." He turned to her, fixed a steady gaze on hers. "And as for what the outside world doesn't know, they select subjects who are insignificant to society—those who won't be missed—and they do research on them." His skull ached with pain still too fresh and familiar even after all this time. "The kind that no one can ever know about."

She held his gaze, her eyes searching his in a way that was suddenly intensely uncomfortable. Regret flared there. "How can you possibly know all this? Did you work in this place?"

He shook his head. "I didn't work there."

Her shoulders lifted in a small shrug. "You had family treated there?" Her breath caught in that little hitch that made her seem all the more vulnerable. "Is that how you know about Research? Did they hurt someone close to you?"

He didn't look away. He wanted to, but he chose not to. She needed to see the truth in his eyes. He needed her trust. "I was a patient there." He allowed those tormenting memories to surface, allowed her to see the agony in his eyes. "In Research."

LUCKY COULDN'T BREATHE for a moment.

Garrett had been a patient in an...*institution*.

"Why?" Lucky's voice echoed hollowly in the thick silence of the kitchen. Garrett flinched. She wished she could take back the solitary word. It took a lot to make a man like him flinch. But she needed to know. Her life and her boss's life depended upon him, it seemed. Understanding all she could about him was essential if she was going to trust him. To help him. "If you feel comfortable talking about it," she added in spite of herself.

All signs of emotion vanished from his face. Rather than maintain eye contact with her, he shifted his attention to making a sandwich. "I was fifteen and what most considered an outlaw. When my mother's boyfriend decided it was time to teach me a lesson, I didn't take it very well."

While he smeared mayonnaise on two slices of bread, Lucky worked on keeping her own painful past out of her head. "You fought back." She hadn't meant to suggest as much out loud but it was instinct.

Lucky Malone had spent most of her childhood doing exactly that—fighting back.

He placed three slices of turkey atop a piece of bread. "If my mom hadn't stopped me I probably would've killed him."

Emotion thickened her throat. "Good thing you listened to her."

He slapped the sandwich together and grabbed it with both hands. "I didn't have a choice." He tore off a big bite, chewed a couple of times, then swallowed. "She stuck a gun to my head."

A hard lump settled like a wad of concrete in Lucky's stomach. "She allowed him to mistreat you then took his side when you'd had enough?" Lucky was intimately familiar with that childhood scenario. Of all the qualities or experiences one person could have in common with another, this was the last one she'd expected to share with this stranger. But every part of her was drawn to him for reasons she didn't comprehend, beyond the fact that he was physically attractive. Maybe their like experience was the answer.

He savored another bite of his sandwich. "Depended upon how deep in the bottle she was."

Lucky reached for the loaf bread. Her hands shook. She should eat, as he suggested. Lunch had been a while ago. Voices from her past reverberated inside her skull. Her mother yelling at her for upsetting her father. Her father threatening to kill them both. Lucky forced the voices away. "I know a little something about that." She passed on the mayonnaise and loaded her bread with turkey. "What about your father?" She nibbled at her sandwich.

"MIA. Never knew him."

That was tough, growing up without a father. Or maybe not. Maybe he was the fortunate one.

"My mother had a penchant for Scotch." He polished off the last of his sandwich. "The brand of Scotch that ensured she died without a penny to her name." He retrieved two sodas from the refrigerator and offered her one. "What about yours?"

She blinked. How could he know that? Was he guessing? Lucky moistened her lips, told herself to breathe. Wait. No. She'd said she knew something about that. He'd made an easy mental leap. "My mother?" she asked in hopes of backtracking.

He ducked his head in a nod of acknowledgment. "I'm not blind, Malone. I couldn't have missed the recognition in your eyes even if you hadn't said anything. You've been all the way there, too."

"Bourbon." She cleared her throat. "My mother loved bourbon. But my father…" She laughed, a dry, humorless sound. "He was an equal opportunity drinker. Didn't matter what kind."

A glimmer of sympathy flashed in his eyes.

Why had she told him that? She shouldn't have volunteered any additional information. Lucky put her sandwich on the counter. Whatever appetite she'd had was gone now. Her palms started to sweat. What was she doing? There were plans to be made.

"You mentioned timing being crucial. What time are we doing this?" Her heart began moving in that unnaturally swift rhythm.

"Ten-fifteen. You need to be in place well in advance of third shift."

Lucky glanced at the clock on the wall above the refrigerator. 6:34. Just over three and a half hours. All this time she'd thought they were wasting time and suddenly it felt like there wasn't enough.

"Why don't you explain exactly how we're going to get in that place?" Talking was more comfortable than the thick silence that lapsed every time there was a lull in the conversation.

He downed the soda and wiped his hand over his mouth. "Straight through the front gate."

Confusion marred her brow. "Why would they let us in?" Then she remembered she was supposed to have a badge. "Won't my being with you make them suspicious?"

"I've got that part under control." He turned to walk away.

She interrupted his exit. "Aren't you worried about going back in there?" Had he maintained a relationship with a member of the staff? He'd called the place hell. The idea that he'd been a mental patient at one point—for reasons she still didn't actually know—made her uneasy all over again. Yet, somehow she now instinctively understood that he wasn't a danger to her. He could have killed several times over had that been his goal.

He faced her once more and shrugged. "I'll worry about that when the time comes."

"Your mother committed you after that incident with her boyfriend?" That realization had just dawned in her brain. Too bad it had slipped off her tongue before she'd had time to analyze the thought.

He held her gaze but his eyes looked empty. Did he have the same trouble examining his past the way she did her own?

"Pretty much."

Something else he'd said cut through the confusion. "You were in what they call Research?" The possibilities related to that revelation twisted in her belly.

"That's right."

"But they released you?" The concept didn't mesh with his description of what they did to those patients.

His lips twisted into a crooked smile that despite its lack of amusement gave him a boyish look that tugged at her somehow. She could almost see the boy who had suffered similar atrocities to those she had survived. That part of her that had recognized a kindred soul wanted to reach out to him. To console the kid who'd been abandoned by his own mother.

"Not exactly."

Her eyes widened with disbelief. "You escaped?" A new reality crashed into her thoughts. "Is it safe for you to go back in there?"

"That's irrelevant."

There was no reason to question that statement.

He was going in to attempt the rescue no matter the personal cost.

Surely there was another way.

Chapter Eleven

Victoria Colby-Camp opened her eyes. She blinked once, twice. Still the darkness shrouded her. Where was she? She tried to sit up. Something held her down. Her hands were restrained with straps. Confusion crowded into her foggy brain.

Her heart thudded against her breast bone. Victoria closed her eyes and ordered herself to calm. She drew in a deep breath, held it, then released. Think, Victoria.

More straps held her body against the bed or gurney. Was this recovery? Where was the nurse? Had her procedure gone as expected?

She felt as if she'd been asleep for days. She swallowed, wishing she had water or ice for her dry throat. Someone would surely come soon. The procedure, recovery time included, was only supposed to take two hours. If she was late, Lucas would worry. Jim and her staff would grow concerned as well. She didn't want them to worry. Not until she knew for sure.

Voices whispered through her mind, parting the

lingering grogginess from the anesthesia. *Careful! This is valuable merchandise.* The idea that she was secured with straps nudged at her instincts.

This wasn't recovery.

Was she even still at the clinic?

Where was Lucky?

Victoria's heart started to pound once more.

The specialist she'd come to see at the clinic was highly regarded by his colleagues. The clinic was one of the best. She tugged at the hand restraints. This was wrong…a mistake.

Or a dream. Perhaps she was still asleep.

Victoria moistened her parched lips. She had to stay calm. Whatever had happened, someone would come into the room sooner or later.

Unless she was dead.

Don't be foolish, she told herself. She took another deep breath.

Victoria closed her eyes and inventoried her surroundings as best she could. The room was cold and the scent was sanitized, antiseptic, like most clinics or hospitals.

The darkness was not right, though. The straps weren't right.

Victoria cleared her throat. "Is anyone there?"

Focus was required to hear above the roar of blood in her ears.

"Hello?" she said, her voice still sounding rusty and all too shaky.

The silence surrounding her echoed more loudly than the pulse thundering inside her.

"You're awake."

The deep, male voiced rumbled only inches from her head. A chilling realization coiled the length of her spine.

"Very good," the man said.

Victoria analyzed the voice. It didn't sound familiar.

"I suppose you have a number of questions."

"At least three," Victoria said. She forced her body to relax and her breathing to slow. She had been in unknown circumstances before. "Where is my assistant? She was to pick me up after the procedure." Victoria prayed Lucky and Burt, the agency's driver, were safe.

"I have no interest in your assistant," he offered in that same quiet tone. "I'm certain she has returned to your office since she was unable to find you at the clinic. I imagine she was quite confused when the clinic insisted they had no patient named Victoria Colby-Camp."

Lucky must have been terrified when she returned to the clinic. Fury lit deep inside Victoria. "Who are you and why am I here?"

"I'm afraid I must remain anonymous for now." Feigned regret weighted his voice. "As for why you're here, that would be because I have a very old score to settle with the man you made the mistake of marrying."

"How original of you." More of that fury blazed inside her. "Cowards always take the easy way out. And in the dark, no doubt."

The bastard chuckled. "I've heard what a courageous woman you are."

Fabric rustled as he leaned toward her. She felt his breath brush her cheek. Her lips tightened in disgust.

"I've waited a very long time to find just the right moment for this. And now I look forward to being the one to break you."

Victoria was the one to chuckle then. "I hope you've got plenty of time, sir." She turned her face toward where she sensed his to be. "Because that's going to take a while."

He laughed outright then. "Not to worry. I have all the time in the world. The longer this takes, the more undone your loving husband will become."

Victoria's heart squeezed at the thought. This monster wouldn't have to lay a hand on Lucas to destroy him. All he had to do was end her life. Jim and Lucas would be devastated. Victoria thought of her son, Jim, and her two beautiful grandchildren and her heart wrenched.

Then a sense of calm settled over her. Lucas and Jim would be searching for her even now. "You underestimate my husband, sir. He will find me and then you'll be the one undone."

The man seemed to consider her threat for a moment. "You are quite right about one part, Victoria. He will find you." The sound of a chair shifting signaled he had stood. "One piece at a time."

Chapter Twelve

9:59 p.m.

Two hours had flown by since a local florist's delivery van had arrived with Garrett's contact. Lucky hadn't been able to hear the exchange between Garrett and the man wearing a T-shirt that sported the floral shop logo, but once the van was gone Garrett had come back inside and given her an envelope.

Inside the envelope was a very official-looking Byrd Institute badge bearing the name Larissa Mills and a photo of Lucky. A bad photo. The same one on her Illinois driver's license. She hated that picture. That was the least of her worries just now. Staying alive was top priority. She couldn't help her boss if she was dead.

Garrett had assured her that no one, not even the esteemed director of the institute, would recognize the badge as a fake. Lucky didn't doubt the claim. The Colby Agency didn't do business with anyone who wasn't the best at whatever they did. Plus Mr. Camp had an endless supply of resources at his disposal. She wasn't worried about the authenticity of the badge.

Holding that badge in her hand prompted a harsh, icy reality to creep deep into her bones. Garrett was totally serious. His rescue plan was going down. He was risking his life to do this. That reality ached through her.

"You're certain this is the only way?" There was no backup. Garrett insisted the institute's security would be monitoring activities around the facility. There was no way to predict the range. Therefore, they were on their own.

Garrett looked up from his phone. He'd been exchanging messages with someone for the past ten minutes. "We're fifteen minutes from moving into position." The frown furrowing his brow warned that he wasn't happy that she'd asked that particular question. "We've been over every step. If you had questions, a couple of hours ago would've been the time to ask."

Lucky had learned something about this seemingly cold, distant man over the course of the afternoon and evening. He didn't appear to care whether he survived this rescue operation or not. There were no exit plans for him. He'd given Lucky detailed instructions on how to get out once she'd found Mrs. Colby-Camp. He would leave his cell phone for her and she was to call the number he'd made her memorize as soon as she and Victoria were out of the tunnel. She would receive further instructions at that point.

And all of that hinged on whether or not she found her boss. Lucky was terrified that she wouldn't be able to locate her and then get her out safely. Thankfully there were no cameras inside the institute other than those at the building's entry points, none of which they would be using. Dr. Byrd wanted no recorded evidence of the goings-on inside the institute. From what Garrett had told her the man had good reason for concealing his evil deeds.

Clearly Garrett had misunderstood her question about whether or not there was another way. Lucky threaded her fingers through her hair and gathered her patience. She was worried about *him*. He'd covered all the bases for her. "What will he do to you?" Garrett hadn't elaborated on the horrors he'd suffered in this place, but her vivid imagination had filled in the blanks a little too well.

Garrett removed his wallet and all other personal items from his pockets. "He'll want to know why I'm here." He opened a cabinet door and started tucking those personal items on the highest shelf. "Where I've been. What I've been up to, yada yada."

Lucky gestured to the cabinet. "Why are you leaving your stuff?" She noticed he hadn't removed the weapon from the waistband of his jeans.

"I don't want to give them any ammunition." He closed the cabinet door. "They're going to have to work for whatever they get. My name, address, etcetera, will take some digging to uncover."

Lucky frowned. "But they know your name."

He locked his gaze onto hers with an unrelenting heaviness that spanned the distance between them. "They know who I used to be."

"You changed your name." She had wanted to do that so many times. To erase who she was and start over.

"I changed everything." He looked away then but she could feel the tension radiating off him.

Lucky hugged her arms around herself. "They'll torture you for that information. For where you've been. Who you've told." A new fist of fear rammed into her sternum. "And why you're back."

"They will." He checked the time on the wall clock. Then his gaze settled on her. "The same way they'll torture you if you get caught."

Uncertainty attempted to hammer away at her courage. Lucky wrestled it aside and squared her shoulders. "I'm aware of that." She understood the risk. She had no choice. The operation had been sanctioned by Mr. Camp. Pride welled inside her. This operation scared her a little, yeah. But the idea that the agency felt she could handle an assignment of such importance gave her courage. Garrett had explained that this was the most feasible option for a safe, speedy rescue. Since his orders were coming from Mr. Camp she had to trust that. She'd gotten past her concerns about whether Mr. Camp had actually sent him. He would never risk so much otherwise.

"Are you sure about that?"

He moved closer to her. Rather than spout an in-

stant yes, Lucky held her breath. He stopped, the
toes of his shoes pressed against the toes of hers,
and stared straight into her eyes. He looked for a long
time, searching for the doubt.

"Yes," she insisted. Her voice wobbled just a little,
annoying the heck out of her. But he was close, really
close. Having him so near caused the strangest flut-
tering in her chest. Not to mention that stir of restlessness that was so totally unexpected.

"If they catch you, they'll try psychological tactics
first."

She held his gaze without blinking. "That's to be
expected."

"Then they'll move on to something like…" He
shrugged those wide shoulders. "Electrical shock
treatments or maybe a well-placed incision."

This time she flinched. "I won't get caught."

His brown eyes bore into hers for enough time
to make her shift nervously. "If you do get caught,
just make sure they don't find out why you're really
there. Your boss's value will go down substantially if
the risk of holding her goes up too much. As long as
Byrd believes no one is aware of her presence, she's
an asset for whatever he has planned."

"I won't tell." Lucky wanted to shake her head for
emphasis but his eyes held her still. "No matter what
they do to me."

For a single second his gaze lowered to her lips.
Her throat tightened and she couldn't resist checking
out his. His mouth was wide, his lips full. He had

nice lips, she realized for the first time. Kissing him would be interesting. She'd never been kissed by a man with lips like that. How long had it been since she'd been kissed at all? Years. Lucky Malone had trouble making that leap from friends to lovers. For the first time in a very long time she wanted to no matter that he was basically a total stranger.

"I hope you're as brave as you think you are," he said as his gaze settled on hers once more. "A life-and-death situation can steal your courage fast."

A new kind of tension, as old and familiar as her own name, whipped through her. "I know." She'd been in that place once before. The blast of her no-good daddy's shotgun echoed in her ears. At seventeen, Lucky had wondered more than once how she would react if put in a life-or-death scenario. God knew she'd had good reason to ponder the possibility. Would she be able to think? To act with courage?

She had discovered that there wasn't time to think at moments like that. Only to act. Lucky had pulled the trigger instinctively and without hesitation even as she stared into the eyes of her own father. Her mother's screams reverberated inside her skull as if Lucky had only just pulled that trigger. A shudder quaked through her.

"Time to go." Garrett backed away from her and headed for the door. "Leave any personal items here and meet me at the truck."

Lucky cleared her head. She had no personal items with her. She'd left everything but Mr. Camp's package in the agency car. And her cell phone. God only knew what happened to it. The package she'd been supposed to deliver was in the truck, she thought. At some point she would need to look for it.

In the white sneakers Garrett had found for her earlier, she walked out to the truck. The shoes were a size too large but at least they wouldn't stand out once she entered the Byrd Institute.

When she reached the truck, Garrett had gathered any documents or items that pointed to his identity as well as the small package Lucky had been supposed to deliver. At least she knew where it was now. She hadn't opened it. Assuming she survived this rescue, she didn't want a single one of her actions to be disappointing to Mr. Camp.

Garrett handed the items to her. "Hide these inside while I remove the license plate."

Her fingers brushed his as she accepted the bundle he'd collected. He felt warm. She, on the other hand, felt as cold as ice. *You're not afraid,* she silently chanted as she hurried back to the kitchen to stash the stuff.

By the time she was back at the truck, he had removed the license plate and replaced it with the one from the car parked behind the house. Smart idea. Of course the enemy could track down his identity through the vehicle's identification number. But that would take time. Like he said, he wasn't going to make it easy for them. Her respect for his preparation skills expanded a little more.

Lucky stared at the truck bed as best she could with only the moonlight. "You're sure this part will work?"

Garrett swiped his palms together before bracing his hands on his hips. "You've asked me that twice already. The time for second thoughts has passed, Malone. It's time to go."

She'd asked a perfectly logical question with good reason. Who had a hiding place built into the bed of his truck? He'd rolled the flexible bed liner back and there it was: a small trap door that opened to a two foot by four foot by eighteen inches deep box. She'd looked under the truck when he'd first told her how their entrance into the facility was going down. The hidden compartment seemed camouflaged well enough. A person would have to know it was there or it would be missed entirely during any sort of visual search.

"Remember," he said, drawing her attention to him, "once we're inside those gates, there's nothing I can do to help you. You'll be on your own with no weapon and no means of communication at your immediate disposal."

"But you said you were leaving your cell in the hole," she reminded him.

"That's right. But you can't take it past the garage. It's too risky." Garrett gestured for her to climb into the bed of the truck. "When you do make your call, keep it short," he warned. "They monitor all transmissions."

Great. "Okay."

With his assistance, Lucky stepped up onto the rear bumper and climbed into the bed of the truck. With a big, bolstering breath, she started to get into the box but she stopped. This was crazy but...

She turned to him. Seeing his face clearly in the dark wasn't necessary. She could imagine the what-the-hell-now expression lined into his face. Before she lost her courage she leaned down and kissed him on the cheek. Just a brush across his beard-stubbled jaw. Warmth rushed through her even as she wanted to kick herself for doing something so utterly foolish.

"What was that for?"

Lucky was enormously thankful that it was dark because her face felt on fire with humiliation. "I... wanted to thank you now." She dragged in a shaky breath. "In case...things don't go as planned."

"In that case." He stepped up on the bumper, towering over her.

Before she could grasp his meaning, he grabbed her by the shoulders and kissed her hard on the mouth. Lucky resisted at first then she melted into him...into the kiss. The pressure from his mouth softened. His tongue slid across her lips, she opened. His arms tightened around her, crushing her against his chest.

He stopped. Set her aside and said, "You're welcome."

Lucky watched, in shock or something along those lines, as he jumped back down.

"Get in," he ordered. "We have a schedule to keep.

Still rattled, Lucky settled into the box, which definitely was not made for human cargo. The awkward position she had to get into would have her muscles cramping in a hurry. She hoped she wouldn't have to be in here long.

"Find your boss quickly," he said, hesitancy in his voice, "and get out of there."

She nodded, her lips on fire from his kiss. Uncertainty and fear had crowded into her throat, making it impossible to speak. Or maybe it was that other whirlwind of sensations. Focus. She could do this. She had to do this.

He removed the battery from his cell and handed both to her before closing the door. She listened as he rolled the bed liner back into place. The confined space went totally black. She closed her eyes and blocked the memory of his kiss. They were going in.

She could seriously have used a flashlight.

DAKOTA BACKED OUT of the drive and pointed his truck toward the institute. His heart rammed hard against his sternum, making his blood roar in his ears.

He wished he could attribute it to what he was about to do, but right this second it was about that damned kiss. Dakota shook his head. He had definitely gone over the edge.

"Get it together." He had a job to do.

In the past several hours he'd come to an en-
lightening conclusion. He wasn't just doing this for
Keaton. He was doing it for himself. This was the
one demon he'd never conquered. The one he'd ran
hard and fast to escape. His entire adult life had been
a complex map of lies, one elaborate fabrication after
the other.

It was past time to face it once and for all, regardless of the outcome.

Dakota shifted into first and let out on the clutch.
He rocketed forward, shifting through the gears as
instinctively as breathing. When he topped the rise
in the road he pushed the accelerator to the floor.

He picked up the bottle of Jack Daniels whiskey
he'd taken from the house and twisted off the top. He
chugged a generous gulp, then splashed some of the
distinctive smelling whiskey on his shirt. Slapped it
on his face like aftershave.

With a flick of his wrist, he tossed the bottle onto
the floorboard and braced for his entrance strategy.

As he approached, two members of security
stepped out of the guard shack. Dakota didn't slow.

Security waved and yelled, but he ignored them.

He just kept driving, straight into the gate.

The impact of metal against metal sent sparks
flying through the air. Bursting through the gates,
Dakota gripped the steering wheel, braced himself
and slammed on the brakes.

Folks had tried this maneuver before. The third

security staffer in the shack would hit the open button at the last possible minute, lessening the damage to the gates.

The truck skidded to a jarring halt.

Security surrounded him, and with weapons aimed at his head, they ordered him to get out of the truck.

"Showtime," he mumbled to himself.

Dakota pulled on the door latch and stumbled out of the truck, hitting the ground face-first.

Security immediately moved in on him.

"What's going on?" He slurred the words. "Where is Dr. Byrd?" he demanded brokenly. "I need to see Dr. Byrd! He's the only one who can help me!"

Two of the guards pulled him to his feet. He swayed drunkenly. "I need Dr. Byrd," he repeated.

"You should be careful what you wish for, buddy," one of the guards threatened.

Dakota glanced back at the truck. Malone was on her own now. He hoped like hell she was stronger than she looked. And that Keaton knew what he was doing.

LUCKY'S MUSCLES ached. Twice she'd had to concentrate hard to relax a muscle that had started to cramp. What was taking so long?

She would be sore come tomorrow. The crash through the gates had sent her nose flat against metal. She should have been braced. Garrett had warned her about his planned dramatic entrance, so she had known the crash was coming.

God, she hoped he was okay.

The truck's engine started again after sitting idle for at least half an hour.

Lucky held her breath and listened for voices.

The truck rolled forward.

About time, she thought. Garrett had said that security would take his vehicle to the maintenance garage. She would need to wait until the truck had been parked and everyone was gone before she could climb out. If she made her move too quickly, she would be done for before she even started. She would end up a prisoner of this place and absolutely no good to her boss.

This place. The Byrd Institute—home of the mentally ill. Those whose cases presented the rarest of challenges and those with whom no one wanted to be bothered. The castoffs. Perfect candidates for unethical research.

The idea that Mrs. Colby-Camp was in here somewhere made Lucky sick to her stomach.

Mr. Camp was no doubt beside himself.

Lucky wished they could have stormed the place, cops and Colby investigators kicking butt. But that kind of operation left too much room for a leak or forewarning. If the bad guys got any advance warning whatsoever, Mrs. Colby-Camp could be killed or moved. They couldn't take that risk. This had to be a sneak attack.

An unexpected invasion.

Garrett was the distraction. Emotion tightened her throat. Don't go there. Stay on task. The hope was that Byrd and his security staff would be so focused on Garrett that no one would pay particular attention to Lucky wandering the corridors.

She had to make her way through the underground tunnel from the maintenance garage to the hospital's basement. The tunnel would lead directly into the janitorial and laundry facilities. The tunnel had been built for receiving supplies. Outsiders were only allowed to deliver goods to the guard shack at the gate. All deliveries were brought to this building for inspection. Only Byrd's handpicked staff moved the goods into the institute.

Once in the basement of the institute, she would get a set of scrubs from the stacks of freshly laundered uniforms. She would clip on her badge and go find Mrs. Colby-Camp and get her out.

All without getting caught.

At least that was the plan.

The truck stopped moving. A loud, grating, metal-on-metal screech filled the air for about ten seconds. The truck rolled forward, stopped again and this time the engine shut off.

Voices.

She strained to make out the words and sounds. Shuffling around in the cab. The raising and lowering of the hood. The truck shifted as someone climbed into the bed. She held her breath.

"Check underneath," a male voice shouted.

Sheer terror ripped through her body.

Seconds ticked off like the countdown to an execution.

"Nothing here." The truck shifted again as the man climbed out.

"Clear below."

"We'll wait and see what Mr. Byrd wants to do with the truck."

Lucky almost fainted with relief. She strained to hear the sounds that would confirm their departure. Their voices faded and a loud grinding indicated the overhead door to the building had closed.

Not about to take any chances, she waited.

At first she tried counting off the minutes but then she just decided to make her move. She pushed at the small door on her hiding space. Garrett had made her do it twice just so she'd understand how hard she would need to push to successfully move the rubber liner covering the bed of the truck as well as the small door.

She grunted with the effort but finally the bed liner plopped out of the way. With the door pushed open, she climbed out. The garage was dark and deserted, only the exit lights providing any illumination.

Closing the door was simple. Getting the bed liner laid out exactly right in the near darkness not so much so. When she felt satisfied that the bed of the truck looked as it had when the two men had left it here, she climbed out of the truck and took a moment to get her bearings.

Once she was in the tunnel, anything could happen. Hopefully she wouldn't run into anyone before reaching the main building.

Moving cautiously in the scarce light, she checked the first door she encountered. Locked. Fear that they would all be locked and that getting out would be impossible pummeled her chest. He'd said the door to the tunnel was near the rear of the building. There was no reason to keep it locked since it didn't access the outside.

The second door was also locked. It couldn't be unlocked without a key. Finally, the knob on the third door turned.

This could be it.

She eased the door open. Her heart stumbled. This door led to the outside. She wasn't supposed to go outside and risk being seen. This door was not supposed to be unlocked.

Before she could pull the door closed her gaze swept over the massive limestone building that loomed across the landscaped grounds. Hundreds of exterior lights spotlighted the forbidding structure, making it look all the creepier.

How would she ever cover that entire building?

Telling herself there was no room for doubt, she forced her legs to move.

She eased the door shut and felt her way to the next door. It opened without resistance. Beyond the door the lighting was dim but at least it wasn't completely dark. She peered at the stairs that descended to a level under the ground. This was definitely the way she was searching for. She entered the stairwell and moved cautiously down the steps.

Her heart pounded so hard she could scarcely breathe. Once she reached the tunnel she relaxed just a little. She could see for a fair distance and the tunnel was clear, as she'd hoped. Moving more quickly, she made it to the other end without incident. She pressed her ear to the door and listened. Hearing only silence, she reached for the knob. But her hand shook. She squeezed it into a fist, then, ignoring the fear trying to filter in, opened her fingers and wrapped them around the knob.

The huge janitorial services room was deserted. The rack of fresh blue scrubs waited on the other side of the room, just as Garrett had said. Lucky looked through the scrubs until she found her size.

She stripped off her bloody clothes and wiggled into the scrubs. After she'd clipped on the badge that identified her as a certified nurse's aid, she hid her clothes and finger combed her hair.

"Okay." Two steps down. Two to go.

Lucky approached the door that would lead into the corridor. Once she was out there she would start to encounter staff members. Garrett had given her the layout of the facility. Unfortunately all that information came with a large caveat—if nothing had changed in the past decade or so.

If she ran into someone, what would she say? She could have asked herself that before now. *Get over it, Lucky.* There was no other choice. This was the only way.

Lucky opened the door and stepped out into the corridor.

The sound of rubber soles on well-polished tile abruptly stopped. A man, dressed in black slacks and a white lab coat turned around.

The bottom fell out of Lucky's stomach. Dear God. Barely through the door and she was caught already.

Chapter Thirteen

10:50 p.m.

The hair on the back of Lucas's neck stood on end.

Something had moved in the rearview mirror.

Lucas had his weapon in his hand and leveled on the window in the same instant a face appeared there.

"Jim." Lucas blew out a puff of air and powered the window down. "I could have shot you."

Jim studied him a moment. The faint glow from the streetlight offered just enough illumination for Lucas to make out the same worry and pain on his stepson's face that was tearing him apart inside.

"I'm getting in."

Lucas hit the unlock button as Jim Colby rounded the hood. When he'd settled into the passenger seat, Lucas said, "How did you find me?"

"I knew you were watching Keaton. Since you weren't at the brownstone, I figured you'd be here."

For hours Lucas had watched the brownstone from which the Equalizers operated. The same one Jim had used when the Equalizers had been his shop. Then he'd followed his mark here, to the small bungalow that Maggie James called home. "Keaton came here around eight." He surveyed the bungalow again.

"I dropped by the coffee shop and spoke to Maggie this afternoon," Jim said somberly.

Lucas turned to him. "And?" Jim was too smart to give away Lucas's suspicions. If he'd learned anything useful, Lucas wanted to know. Now.

"She's in deep with Keaton." Jim stared straight ahead, into the darkness. "Her expression when she said his name left no doubt. She hedged giving specific details about him. She knows or suspects some aspect of Keaton. That was very clear."

"Maggie's a good woman." Lucas shook his head. "If something's off with Keaton, she won't deny it for long."

The question Lucas needed to ask next jammed in his throat. Victoria and Lucky had been missing approximately twelve hours now. Tracking his wife's cell phone had proved a bust. All traces of its movements had been wiped beyond the location of an outpatient surgery clinic. But Lucky's phone had not. They had traced her movements to the surgery clinic and then to the drop location. Since neither Victoria nor Lucky had been at that location, they had backtracked to the clinic. Nothing. Lucas had contacted Victoria's personal physician in case he was missing something. An unfamiliar emotion twisted in his gut.

Fear was not a companion he'd ever kept…until now. He despised himself for being so weak.

"We've found nothing," Jim said without Lucas having to ask. "The cops are baffled. It's like they just vanished. Dr. Klein is stunned. The clinic's CEO has found nothing."

Lucas closed his eyes against the agony. Victoria's personal physician, Klein, had recommended her to that clinic, just not for today. Today's appointment had been bogus. The clinic had been closed for remodeling for the past week. No one could explain today's events. Victoria's friend with whom she'd said she would be meeting had not spoken to Victoria. Even more painful, Victoria had scheduled a medical procedure without telling Lucas. Dr. Klein could not disclose the reasons for that appointment. Now she was missing.

But she and Lucky hadn't just disappeared. Someone had taken them. There had been no ransom demand, no triumphant announcement from an old enemy. Nothing.

Keaton had to be involved. Lucas had a feeling about him. One way or another he would find the truth and that would lead him to Victoria.

Chapter Fourteen

Lucky's feet had bonded to the floor. She couldn't run. Her mind had frozen, hindering her ability to utter a single word of explanation. Her lungs had emptied of oxygen.

The man strode straight up to her while she watched in horror.

"Maybe you're new," he snapped impatiently. "This is a nonsmoking facility." He shook his finger in her face. "You're the second staff member I've caught tonight sneaking down here to the maintenance room to smoke." He stared at her badge. "If I catch you again, Ms. Mills, there will be consequences."

The relief Lucky felt was so profound that her knees nearly buckled. "I wasn't smoking," she had the presence of mind to say. She tugged at her scrub top. "I had to change. A patient—"

He waved a hand. "Whatever. I have patients." He lifted a skeptical eyebrow. "I presume you do as well and I know none of those patients are on this floor."

She jerked her head up and down. "Yes, sir."

He executed a one-eighty and stalked away.

Lucky sucked in a breath and slowly turned toward the stairwell that would lead to the upper floors. Garrett had told her to avoid the elevators and stick to the stairs. So far his memory of the institute's floor plan had been spot on.

The soles of the borrowed sneakers squeaked softly on the tile floor. She focused a little harder on making her steps completely silent. The stairwell was still and quiet, nevertheless she listened for half a minute to ensure she was alone. Garrett had explained that the first floor was made up of offices and the lobby. No need for her to nose around there.

It was the next three floors where she'd have to be on her toes.

Lucky bypassed the exit to the first floor and moved more quickly up to the second. She hesitated at the exit and braced for whatever lay beyond the door. Hospital staff, security personnel. Obstacles. Complications. She touched the badge clipped to her scrub top then reached for the doorknob.

Mrs. Colby-Camp was here somewhere and she needed Lucky's help. The longer she hesitated, the more her boss might suffer.

She opened the door and stepped into the long white corridor. Lucky blinked. The corridor was deserted and as silent as a vacant house. Fluorescent lighting glared against the white tile floors. Doors lined the stark white walls. The main corridors on each floor ran north and south with smaller side halls to the east and west. A nurses' station would be located at the two primary corridor intersections. Those were to be avoided if at all possible.

Her heart pounding, Lucky moved to the first door. She opened it quietly and eased inside. The patient was male. Elderly. Lucky relaxed as much as she dared and retraced her steps. The next room was occupied by a woman. Young, Lucky's age maybe. She hoped all the patients were sleeping as the first two were.

By the time she'd checked each of the rooms on the south end of the corridor her confidence had gained a decent foothold. According to Garrett the nurses did rounds at each shift change. Any time now she was going to come face-to-face with one or more. She was new and lost. Where did she get fresh bed linens?

At the intersection of corridors she peeked around the corner, her pulse racing. One nurse, preoccupied with paperwork, sat at the desk.

Lucky checked east and west, then the desk once more before moving through the intersection. When she'd cleared the narrower corridor she dared to breathe again.

She reached for the first door to her right and opened it. Before she could slip inside, a door opened about halfway down the corridor. A nurse stepped out.

The nurse wrote something on the chart in her

hand. Lucky ducked through the door she'd opened, then closed it, holding down the handle so the latch didn't click as it engaged. She froze for a second or two and listened for the nurse's approach. If she'd seen Lucky, she would come to check it out.

The scarce whisper of rubber soles passed in the corridor. Lucky relaxed and moved on.

She covered the entire second floor without running into trouble. She kept a step or two ahead of the two nurses making rounds. Returning to the stairwell, she was relieved to find it deserted like before. One floor down, two to go. At this rate, she would be out of here in no time. Not about to get cocky, she maintained caution as she began her search of the third floor.

This time all of the floor's nurses were at the desks so Lucky moved quickly through the rooms. So far every patient had been sleeping. Lucky hoped her good fortune held out. The patients were mostly adults, only a few who looked younger than twenty. As many women as men and only the occasional one secured to the bed. The facilities were far nicer than she'd expected. A bit sterile but nice. Not at all the house of horrors she'd anticipated.

Lucky checked the corridor and progressed toward the last row of doors. She felt giddy with how smoothly her search was going.

But she hadn't found Mrs. Colby-Camp.

What if they were wrong? What is she wasn't here?

Lucky's stomach twisted. She had to be here. Her cell phone had been tracked to this location.

But if she wasn't…they were wasting valuable time. And Garrett had surrendered himself to this place for nothing. Lucky didn't want to think about what they might be doing to him at this very moment.

Mrs. Colby-Camp was top priority.

Lucky had to find her. Fast. Then she had to help Garrett. As soon as she got her boss to safety, of course. Garrett had given her strict instructions on how to get Mrs. Colby-Camp out. He had actually insisted that Lucky was not to attempt to rescue him, that he had an exit strategy. But she didn't believe him. She had to help him. That fire he started in her belly with that kiss kindled.

Focus, Lucky.

She slipped into the final room on the third floor and closed the door, ensuring the latch reengaged silently. Her chest tightened with anticipation. This could be the one. What if Mrs. Colby-Camp was sedated? She dismissed that worry. That was a bridge she'd just have to cross when she came to it.

Strong arms wrapped around her neck and jerked her backward against a heaving chest. Lucky's hands went to her throat and she tried to pry loose.

"I knew they'd send someone," a male voice growled in her ear. "And here you are."

Lucky resisted the urge to scream.

It was too late for that.

"Why are you here?"

Strapped to a chair in one of the research rooms, Dakota stared into the eyes of the man he'd dreamed of killing for more than a decade. That the old bastard was visibly unsettled by Dakota's appearance made his century. Rather than answer the question Byrd's associates had already asked repeatedly with their fists, Dakota licked the blood from his busted lip and spat in his face.

The old man's muscle-bound associates rushed forward. Byrd held up his left hand while swiping the spittle from his face with his right. "Back off."

"And you were just warming up," Dakota said to the two men who were clearly disappointed. He managed a grin though it burned like hell.

Dr. Byrd stepped away from Dakota. "Move him to the examining table."

Even as his gut twisted with dread, Dakota said, "Now the real fun begins."

Byrd glared at him as his men unstrapped Dakota from the chair. He would not show his apprehension. Not for a second. Byrd enjoyed the fear and helplessness of those he chose to analyze. Dakota wasn't giving him that pleasure.

With Dakota secured to the bed, Byrd dared to approach him once more. Dakota despised cowards and this evil scumbag was definitely a coward.

"I never learned how you escaped." Byrd pursed his lips a moment. "Though I tried. The friends you'd made here were loyal to the very end. I can't imagine why." He shrugged his narrow shoulders. "It's not as if you offered anything in return."

The nurse, Colleen Patrick, and the janitor, Max. Dakota's gut clenched. The only two people in this hellhole who'd treated him like a human. "They couldn't tell you what they didn't know." The snarl echoed in the room. Dakota had run and he hadn't looked back. He'd left the people here without so much as an anonymous tip to help them out of this nightmare.

He was the coward.

But he'd been nothing more than a kid. He'd been fending for himself so long he'd forgotten the concept of providing relief or assistance to others. Even now, what he did for those in need was an assignment, a job.

Whatever compassionate feelings he had possessed died a long time ago at the hands of one of his mother's deadbeat boyfriends.

"Too bad you wasted your time and resources." Dakota curled his damaged lips into a sneer. "You'll never know just how badly your security sucks."

Byrd turned to one of his men. "Prepare him."

Tension rippled through Dakota. Remembered agony followed on its heels. He focused on the white ceiling. Ceilings, walls and floors. Everything about this place was sickeningly white. And yet, this was one of the darkest places on the planet. Dark and hopeless.

"Perhaps an old acquaintance will loosen your

tongue." Byrd smirked. "Few are able to resist after a few minutes of this particular persuasion."

Electrodes were placed in pivotal spots around his skull. Dakota locked his jaw and forced the rest of his body to relax. He'd survived shock treatments before. He could do it again.

When the preparations were completed, Byrd clasped his hands behind his back and studied Dakota. "It's quite a shame. I had high hopes for a breakthrough in your case. Perhaps you could have led a normal life had you cooperated with my treatments."

A laugh burst out of Dakota. "You mean a normal life as a zombie." He'd seen the results of Byrd's treatments. Experimental surgeries, unapproved drug therapies, not to mention the bastard's prized shock therapy. What he did to those patients who had no family or friends was unspeakable. Dakota knew firsthand.

Fury glittered in the doctor's eyes. "There are sacrifices in all fields of research."

"I think maybe those sacrifices are supposed to be voluntary. Made by people of sound mind." The only sacrifice Dakota would like to see right now was one that included a bullet between this evil maniac's eyes.

"Why did you come back?" Byrd demanded.

"I missed you," Dakota tossed at him.

Movement in the corner of his eye warned

that Byrd's associate was reaching for the control console.

Byrd held up a hand, postponing the first wave of current. "Is there someone here who interests you? A patient? A member of my staff?"

Dakota curled his hands into fists and covertly tugged at the straps binding his wrists. A realization burned deep into his brain. He looked straight into the doctor's eyes and said, "You. I came back for you."

The statement felt more real than any he'd made in his entire adult life. Dakota would never truly be free of the past until he'd stopped this monster.

Seemingly intrigued, Byrd again put off the inevitable. "You were like my own son." He shook his head. "You were bright and full of so much potential. I wanted to make you whole. To neutralize those violent outbursts. You must have seen how deeply I care for all my patients. You in particular."

Dakota looked away. "This was the only safe home I ever knew." What a disgusting lie. But he needed a break here. He needed Byrd off guard.

"Then you fared no better as a man," Byrd suggested.

Dakota gave his head a negligible shake. "I sank back into my old ways. Used my ability to wreak havoc and damage to survive."

"It's not too late to correct that pattern. There are measures that can be taken now to neutralize those destructive impulses."

Dakota wanted to laugh at the twisted sincerity in the madman's voice. Instead, he met his gaze. "You really believe it's not too late? You can still help me?" He cleared his throat as if emotion had clogged it. "You know that's why I'm back. This has to end." Damn straight. This whole place had to be brought down. And Dakota was going to do it. Chances of him getting out were slim to none. He might as well make the most out of his final feat.

Byrd took a breath. "Bring him to the critical decision unit." Dr. Byrd turned to leave the room.

"Sir," the associate manning the controls spoke up, "are you sure that's a good idea? He's quite unmanageable when less than fully secured."

Byrd paused at the door and sent a glower at the man. "Then do your job. See that he is adequately secured. I'll need to conduct a full analysis."

A shudder rumbled inside Dakota. Analysis. Code for inhumane testing, mental and physical.

"Of course, sir."

Byrd left the room. The door whooshed to a close behind him, leaving a silence chock-full of tension.

The second man, the one stationed at the foot of the examining table, removed a pair of nylon wrist restraints from his pocket.

"We won't need those," the other announced.

"Dr. Byrd said—"

"I know what he said." The guy lingered at the controls. "Dr. Byrd didn't specify how to secure him."

He smirked. "As long as he's manageable that's what counts." The bastard hit the On switch.

Dakota braced for the fiery current.

Chapter Fifteen

Lucky didn't dare move. Still, the man's arm tightened around her neck as if he wasn't taking any chances on whether she would bolt.

"What took you so long?" he growled close to her ear, impatience or frustration radiating in his tone.

"I…" Lucky swallowed against the choking sensation threatening to cut off her ability to breathe. "I came as quickly as I could." She'd learned from her father that when dealing with uncertainty, it was best to play along as long as possible.

He dragged her deeper into the dark room. Lucky's feet scrambled to stay beneath her. Her fingers instinctively dug more deeply into the man's hairy arm. The urge to fight roared beneath her skin, keeping time with her racing heart.

"I've been protecting the asset," he assured Lucky in a rough whisper. "I wasn't sure how much longer I could maintain my cover."

A new kind of fear leeched into her veins. This was not the institute's security. Could be a good thing…or something way worse.

"You got here in the nick of time."

"I…"

He released her.

Lucky grappled for balance and denied her instinct to run for the door. If this man wasn't security, he was a patient.

Rallying her fading courage, she turned around. A flame flickered to life in front of his face. A lighter.

He nodded toward the flame. "I snatched it from one of the guards." Pride glowed on the man's face.

The poor guy was obviously delusional. He wore a blue print hospital gown. His feet were bare. Whatever was going on inside his head, Lucky was fairly sure that continuing to play along would be the smart thing to do.

"Good idea," she praised. "It'll work just as well as a flashlight." What the heck did she do now?

The man hissed a curse and the flame died. "Not good for long-term use."

"I should carry on with my mission," she ventured. All she had to do was get out of this room without him drawing attention from the nurses who would, in turn, call security. If he insisted on accompanying her she was going to be in trouble.

"Of course," he agreed. "Come with me."

Before Lucky could decide how to react to that order, he reached out and snagged her arm. Lucky resisted the urge to snatch her arm back. Instead, she let him lead her. Her eyes had adjusted to the dark, allowing her to vaguely make out the bed in the middle of the room and a small bedside table. He stopped in front of a door. Closet or bathroom probably.

"Keep quiet," he whispered. "If they hear us we're done for."

He opened the narrow door, then ushered her in front of him. Lucky's pulse tripped. If he was about to shove her into a closet and...

He reached around her and flicked the lighter. The flame cut a path through the darkness of what turned out to be a small bathroom.

He squeezed past her and drew the shower curtain aside. "I told you," he said excitedly. "I kept the asset safe and sound."

Lucky's gaze settled on the tiled shower stall. A woman sat on the tile floor, her knees hugged to her chest and her head down. Strands of silver glistened against her coal-black hair.

Lucky's gasp echoed softly in the tiny room. "Mrs. Colby-Camp."

The woman's head came up.

It was her!

Lucky rushed forward and dropped to her knees in front of the shower. "Are you all right, ma'am?"

The man muttered a curse and the light extinguished.

"Lucky?" Mrs. Colby-Camp's voice sounded thick. "What're you doing here? Did they kidnap you, too?"

"I'll explain later. Right now we have to get out of here." Lucky slid an arm around her boss and urged her to her feet. She leaned heavily against Lucky. "Can you walk?" If she couldn't walk Lucky would have an awful time getting her out of this place.

Before Mrs. Colby-Camp could answer, the man loitering in the doorway said, "They sedated her. That's the only reason I could get her out of her room. They figured she wasn't going anywhere so they didn't leave a guard."

"Where were they keeping her?" The lighter came on again. Lucky blinked.

"Next room." He nodded toward the wall behind Lucky. "I heard the enemy threatening her. I knew she was a hostage."

Who was this man? "You did an excellent job, sir." Was he actually crazy or was he someone this institute had used in the experiments Garrett spoke of? Did he need rescuing, too?

"That's colonel to you, young lady," he said proudly, shoulders reared back. "Colonel Henry Marshall, United States Air Force, Retired."

"Colonel," Lucky acknowledged. She turned to her boss. "Ma'am, put your arm around my waist and hang on." How in the world was she going to get out of here when Mrs. Colby-Camp could scarcely stand? How much time did she have before someone came around looking for her?

The colonel stepped back from the door and gestured for them to follow. Lucky guided her boss through the narrow doorway. The lighter went out again.

"You should try to escape, Lucky," her boss murmured. "It's too dangerous for you to do this."

"Mr. Camp sent me." Saying those words chased away the uncertainty plaguing her. Lucky could do this. Mr. Camp was depending on her.

"He'll be back for her in a few hours," the colonel said. "He's taking her away from here so he can do very bad things. You must not be captured."

Mrs. Colby-Camp shivered.

"Who's coming?" Lucky asked. She wished she could see the colonel's face. "Is it Dr. Byrd?"

"I don't know his name," he said. "But there's no time to waste. You should hurry."

Fear tied another knot in her belly. He was right. She firmed her hold on her boss. It was the how that was going to be dicey.

"I'll create a diversion," the colonel said. He walked to the door separating his room from the corridor and opened it just enough to peek out.

Lucky guided her boss forward until they stood behind him. "Will that put you at risk?" The poor man had already taken several as far as Lucky could tell.

"I can take care of myself, soldier." He thrust the lighter at her. "You might need this."

Lucky drew in a bolstering breath and accepted the lighter. Any kind of light was better than none. "Thank you, colonel."

"Stay out of sight until you hear me shout the code word. I know all the nurses on this floor. When they're all gathered around me trying to control the situation, I'll give you the go-ahead. *Scramble.*"

If Lucky could make it to the stairwell, the odds of escaping were greatly increased. "I understand." She could do it. Definitely.

"Hold your position." He eased the door open wider.

"I won't forget your bravery, colonel," Mrs. Colby-Camp said, her voice uncharacteristically weak. "I am in your debt, sir."

The light peeking through the gap in the door spotlighted the colonel's two-fingered salute. "My pleasure, ma'am." Then he opened the door wider and slipped out.

Lucky eased the door nearly closed behind him. She chewed her lip, leaning closer to the narrow opening. Her head was spinning. She should be terrified, but she wasn't. Not really. The fear was there, but somehow it stayed at bay. What had just happened here? Who was this Colonel Marshall? Images of the way Garrett had come to her rescue early this morning replayed in her mind. To run into two heroes in one day was unusual to say the least. Maybe fate had decided to give her a break.

"You need to be aware," her boss said, "that the man who had me brought here is extremely dangerous. If he finds us, he'll kill you."

That terror loitering on the fringes of her consciousness crept closer. "Did you recognize him?" Shouting in the corridor near the nurse's desk had her heart rate climbing and her attention shifting back to the door.

"No, but he's an old enemy of Lucas's. That alone guarantees he's dangerous. If he catches us, he'll have no mercy." She released a weary breath. "I can't allow you to take such a risk."

Lucky kicked back the fear. "Then we won't let him catch us."

"However you got in here," the boss argued, "your odds of escaping that way are considerably more likely without me slowing you down."

Above the other shouting she distinctly heard the word *Scramble*.

"There's no time," Lucky said as she moved her boss into the corridor. She took a deep breath and hoped the colonel knew what he was doing.

She didn't breathe again until they were well down the corridor. Moving was slower than she'd like, but Mrs. Colby-Camp was weak and a little wobbly. Before reaching each landing, Lucky stilled and listened for company. So far the stairwell remained clear. The next step was to get back to the truck. Garrett's cell was in the hole where she'd hidden. Lucky had memorized the number she was to call.

Help was supposed to be close.

Really close, Lucky hoped.

Twice they had to stop for Mrs. Colby-Camp to rest. When they made it to the basement level,

Lucky wanted to check the corridor before exposing her boss.

"Rest here a moment." Lucky ushered her boss to the wall beneath the stairs.

"What're you doing?" Worry cluttered Mrs. Colby-Camp's face.

"Just making sure the coast is clear." Lucky managed a smile. "I'll be right back."

Lucky took a second to compose herself. She had the uniform and the badge, so she would be fine. She opened the door and looked out.

The corridor was clear.

Her pulse thudding, Lucky returned to the stairwell. "It's clear."

Mrs. Colby-Camp nodded.

Moving down that open corridor at such a slow pace had Lucky's nerves frazzled by the time they reached the door to the laundry and maintenance room.

Lucky opened the door and got Mrs. Colby-Camp inside. As she started to close the door she froze. She inhaled deeply. What was that smell?

Smoke. Cigarette smoke.

Lucky touched her finger to her lips. Mrs. Colby-Camp nodded her understanding.

Think!

Lucky carefully closed the door, ensuring the latch didn't click. She ushered her boss behind the nearest rack of laundry. After squaring her shoulders, Lucky smoothed a hand over her scrub top and followed the smell of smoke.

A woman dressed in the same type of scrubs as Lucky jumped and made a little sound of surprise.

"Sorry." Lucky made a face that reflected her regret. "I came to do the same thing." She reached into the pocket of her scrub pants and pulled out the lighter the colonel had given her. She huffed. "Dang it, I forgot my—"

"Here." The blonde woman who looked to be about thirty and whose badge sported the name Nita Sparks handed Lucky her pack of cigarettes.

Lucky sighed. "Thanks." She took one from the pack and passed it back. Careful not to draw the smoke into her lungs—she'd learned that trick back in high school when she'd tried being cool—she lit the cigarette.

"You new?" Nita asked.

Lucky nodded. "Just started. Which floor are you on?" she inquired before Nita could.

"Two. You?"

"Third." She took another pretend draw. "One of our old guys who thinks he's still in the military freaked out a few minutes ago. I'm glad it was time for my break."

Nita dropped her spent cigarette, scrubbed it out with the toe of her shoe then slid it between the bars of the large drain cover in the floor. "That happens when they don't take their meds." She gave Lucky a knowing look. "You have to watch 'em close. They'll pretend they've swallowed it then spit it out when you leave the room. Most of 'em are harmless, but there's a few who can be pretty violent."

"Oh, yeah. I was warned about that."

Nita tucked her cigarettes under her scrub top. "Gotta get back on the floor. See ya 'round."

"Sure thing." Lucky watched her walk away, scarcely resisting the urge to follow her. When she heard the soft click of the door's latch, she tossed her cigarette in the same manner as the other woman, made a face at the nasty taste in her mouth, then hurried back to where she'd left her boss.

"We're clear now."

Mrs. Colby-Camp looked tired but relieved. Lucky sure hoped the help that was supposed to be close would arrive soon. If the man who'd arranged Mrs. Colby-Camp's abduction still had plans for her then chances were the sedative wasn't harmful. He could be looking for her right now.

Getting through the tunnel was fast and, thankfully, uneventful. Once in the massive garage, Lucky moved more slowly. There was very little light and she couldn't use the lighter and hold her boss, too. Garrett's truck was a site for sore eyes.

"Rest here a moment." She left the boss leaning against the truck and climbed into the bed of the truck. Using the lighter for visibility, she moved the bed liner and opened the door to the hidden compartment.

Her fingers couldn't seem to put the cell's battery

in place, turn it on and punch in the numbers quickly enough. A man's voice answered on the first ring. She didn't recognize it, but since she had to keep the call short, there was no time to ask his identity. Garrett had warned her that transmissions were monitored.

"It's Lucky Malone. We're in position."

"You know what to do," the man said. "Your extraction is in ten minutes."

Lucky frowned. "Wait, what about Garrett? He's still in there."

"He can take care of himself for now. I'll make arrangements for him later."

No. That wasn't acceptable. "They'll torture him." Or worse.

"You have your orders."

No way. "She'll be here," Lucky said, before she had time to second-guess herself. "I'm going back for Garrett."

The man said something else but Lucky didn't listen. She turned off the phone and removed the battery as Garrett had instructed.

She climbed out of the truck and joined her boss. "Help will be here in ten minutes. But until then I have to hide you."

Mrs. Colby-Camp shook her head. "Something's very wrong here. Was that Lucas?"

"There's no time to explain." Lucky helped her boss to the truck's tailgate. "I have to hurry or Garrett might be badly hurt or worse." She couldn't believe they were just going to leave him to fend for himself for now. The Colby Agency didn't usually work that way. As her boss said, this whole operation was a little off somehow.

"Who is this Garrett you're talking about? Have you spoken to Jim or Simon?"

There was no time. Lucky climbed into the bed of the truck and reached down to assist her boss. "I'll tell you everything when this is over. Please," she urged when her boss still hesitated, "there's no time."

Mrs. Colby-Camp took Lucky's hand and climbed in. Lucky used the lighter to show her the hiding place. Mrs. Colby-Camp didn't ask any more questions or hesitate. She climbed in and struggled into position.

"I know it's not very comfortable, but you won't be in here long. I'm going to cover you now."

"Lucky."

She flicked the lighter so she could see her boss's face. "Yes."

"Whatever this man Garrett has told you, I'm certain that Lucas didn't put you in this position. You need to be very careful."

Lucky promised she would, then quickly closed the door to the box and put the bed liner in place.

She hurried to the door that would take her back into the tunnel. Then she hesitated. That her boss was so certain about Mr. Camp not being involved unnerved her to some degree. Garrett insisted that Lucas was running this operation. Would he lie to her?

Why save her life, then lie?

She shook it off. Didn't really matter right now. Garrett needed her help. She couldn't leave without going after him.

He'd already done the same for her.

Chapter Sixteen

"What did you do?" Byrd demanded.

Dakota kept his head hanging down. After they'd finished playing, Byrd's associates had dragged him to the critical decision unit and dumped him into a chair. He'd only been semiconscious for part of the journey. Even now he felt somewhat disconnected and lethargic but he was aware of the goings-on in the room. The longer he could keep that knowledge to himself, the longer it would be before he was secured.

"I gave him a few volts to keep him manageable. He'll live."

Bastard, Dakota spat out silently. A few volts. Yeah, right.

Truth was, the jerk was right about the last. Dakota had been through those "management" sessions plenty of times when he'd been a resident of this hellhole. And he'd lived.

"Move him to the examining table and secure him."

Hands grabbed Dakota and hauled him to his feet.

He lolled his head, relaxed his body completely, leaving his weight to drag against their efforts.

Pounding on the door almost made Dakota flinch.

"Dr. Byrd, there's an emergency that requires your attention."

This voice was new. Dakota listened as he was heaved onto the examining table.

"I am not to be disturbed," Byrd snarled at the newcomer. "I'm certain you can handle any problems with the patients. Now get out."

"Sir, it's—"

"Damn you, Byrd, what have you done?"

Another new voice. This one mad as hell. Dakota fought the urge to open his eyes. The two tasked with his security had apparently stopped to watch the show. Maybe he was about to get a lucky break.

"What're you talking about?" Byrd demanded.

"She's missing," the newest one to arrive said. "Victoria is not in her room."

Dakota resisted the urge to smile. Lucky had done it. She'd found her boss and made a run for it. Damn, he was impressed. He hadn't been sure she'd had it in her. Any time now Keaton would breach the compound and drive both Lucky and the head of the Colby Agency out of here. Good. Mission accomplished.

"That's impossible," Byrd roared.

"Find her or our deal is off. And you know what that means. I will destroy you."

Silence thickened in the air.

"Come," Byrd said. "You stay with him."

The rush of footsteps combined with the fading angry demands of the man who'd announced Victoria was missing proved too much for Dakota to ignore. He had to take the chance and look.

Only one member of security remained in the room with him. The guy shut the door. Dakota closed his eyes and waited for his approach.

The guard straightened Dakota's right arm and prepared to fasten the strap around his wrist.

Dakota made his move. He came up with his left fist, connecting solidly with the man's jaw. The guard stumbled back. Dakota jumped to his feet and plowed into the guy, ramming him against the wall.

They tumbled to the floor in a heap of plunging fists and butting heads. Dakota took a blow to the jaw and got his head banged against the floor, but he managed to head-butt the guy's nose. That gave him the upper hand for a split second. It was all the time Dakota needed. He pinned him to the floor and manacled his hand before he snagged his weapon. Dakota pressed his forearm against the guy's throat.

The guard flailed, held out longer than Dakota had expected. But eventually he surrendered to the lack of oxygen. Dakota let up on his throat rather than finishing him off. All he needed was him unconscious.

Dakota relieved him of his high-tech walkie-talkie. While he was at it he grabbed the guy's badge in case he needed it for getting through a door. He checked the corridor and headed for the exit. The research rooms and critical decision unit were behind a set of security doors marked Authorized Personnel Only. Once through those doors he could be at the tunnel in three minutes flat.

He hesitated at an intersection of corridors. Two nurses were seated at the desk. Dakota waited long enough to confirm that the two were deep enough in conversation for him to move. He made the move and headed for the exit doors that stood between him and getting out of here. If he was damned lucky no one would be on the other side.

He swiped the badge's magnetic strip across the scanner and the doors opened.

The corridor was empty. Evidently all of security was attempting to track down Victoria Colby-Camp.

The walkie-talkie crackled. He held it close to his ear and listened. The gate guards were calling in a security breach. A blue pickup had just crashed through the gates, escaping the compound.

Lucky and her boss were out of here.

Dakota shook his head. The lady had definitely proven a hell of a lot more resourceful and stronger than he'd first concluded.

More squawking on the walkie-talkie warned Dakota that his escape had been discovered and that security had been sent after the escapees in the blue truck. The next warning made him smile. The male escapee, Gage Eaton, was now suspected to be driving the truck; he was armed and dangerous.

Eaton...the name Dakota had been born to.

He clenched his jaw and kicked the echo of history from his brain.

He would never be that pathetic person again.

The final stretch of corridor lay between him and the door to freedom.

Then it opened.

Dakota halted dead in his tracks. He palmed the weapon he'd borrowed from the guard. Then he saw the person who'd opened it.

"Malone?" What the hell?

She jumped, clutched at her chest. Then she flung herself at him. Her arms went around his neck. "Oh, God, I was afraid you were dead!"

Dakota stiffened. "I'm fine."

"Thank God," she muttered into his chest. "I was so worried."

He couldn't help himself. His arms went around her. "It's okay." What the hell was he doing? They didn't have time for this.

She abruptly drew back and looked up at him. "How did you get away?"

"Never mind that," he snapped, pulling free of her touch. She made him want things he never expected to want again. "Why aren't you with Victoria?" Malone wasn't supposed to be here. Getting out was going to be tough enough without his having to worry about her.

"Never mind that," she smart-mouthed, using his own words against him. "How do we get out of here?"

For sure they weren't getting out right now. Security would be crawling all over the place.

He grabbed her hand. "We have to lay low until the heat settles."

"Why can't we—"

She didn't get to finish. He hauled her back through the door she'd just exited.

He considered their limited options. Heating and cooling units, industrial-sized laundry equipment.

There was just one place they *might* be safe.

He lugged her over to the row of carts filled with soiled linens. He emptied a cart. "Climb in."

Still obviously confused, she didn't argue. Once she was in the cart, he moved some of the dirty laundry to the next cart. Then he climbed in with her and pulled the rest of the laundry into the cart with them.

"We need to be buried."

"Better to be buried with cotton than dirt," she muttered as she helped him to pull the sheets and towels over them.

"Now we wait."

She sighed. "How long do we have to wait?"

"Until we have another option."

The more time that passed with Byrd's people unable to locate their prey, the more lax the security would become. Eventually someone would decide that Dakota had indeed escaped in his truck along with Victoria Colby-Camp and an unidentified perpetrator. Then he and Malone could make a run for it.

Except that wouldn't stop Byrd.

Fury heated in Dakota's veins. He wasn't leaving this time without putting a stop to the madman's so-called research. Last time Dakota had been a kid. Saving himself had been his only priority.

Not this time.

"They hurt you."

Malone's statement dragged him back to the immediate situation. They'd had no choice but to cram and curl their bodies into this thing. She'd faced the back of the cart while he had snuggled up behind her. Until she'd spoken he had been able to ignore the way her bottom felt nestled against him.

His brain and body homed in on the wrong details, like how firm yet soft her body felt, the way her heat seeped into him. Still, he managed to say, "What about you?"

"The uniform kept me out of trouble."

"Good."

She wasn't finished with her questions. He felt the tension in her body.

"What you did," she began softly, "kept me safe and gave me the opportunity to save my boss." She hesitated. "I'm sorry you had to go through…this."

He didn't need her sympathy. What he needed was to get the hell out of here and she had complicated that strategy. "You were supposed to leave with your boss. What went wrong?"

"Nothing went wrong."

She was annoyed now. Her body had stiffened as if being this close to him made her all the angrier.

He pressed the issue. "If nothing went wrong, why are you here?" He didn't need her going soft.

"I came back for you," she said tightly. "Your contact was just going to leave you here. Someone had to rescue you."

He laughed a low, hollow sound. "You believed I needed rescuing? I was on my way out when you got in the way."

Malone attempted to put some distance between them. It didn't work. "You told me what they did to you before. I didn't want that to happen again."

He opened his mouth to say something sarcastic and cutting but all he managed was, "Too late."

She didn't say anything to that. Good. He didn't need her sympathy or her misguided heroics.

"I know how that feels."

Why didn't she just give it a rest? He needed to focus on the current situation. Listen for the enemy.

"My father beat me and my mother every time he got frustrated at work or ticked off at one of his drinking buddies."

She said the words so softly that he'd had to huddle closer to hear. He didn't want to listen but couldn't help himself.

"All those years." She let go a heavy breath. "She

never once tried to stop him or tried to run away. I couldn't understand why she didn't fight back. If not for herself, for me. What kind of mother doesn't at least try to protect her child?"

When she got old enough she protected herself. He hadn't known the details but he'd read about the shooting when he'd ran a check on her. Hearing those details, Dakota's respect for Malone deepened despite his best efforts not to feel anything at all. That usually wasn't a problem for him.

"One day I'd had enough," she continued, her voice distant and barely audible. "So I got that shotgun he liked to scare us with and I shot him dead." She made a soft sound, almost a laugh. "Funny thing was, everyone thought I did it for my mother. The local newspaper called me a hero for saving my mother from a drunken abuser. Truth was, I was saving myself. I wasn't going to let that no-good piece of dirt hit me ever again."

Dakota had been there, too. Only, when he fought back his mother had sent him here. Looked like he and Malone were two of a kind. Hell of a thing to have in common.

There were comforting words he could have said to her after such a painful confession. But he couldn't stop rolling over the idea of just how differently they had turned out. Similar childhood tragedies. No one to count on but themselves. Yet they were as different as day and night now. He'd seen firsthand the extremes Malone was willing to go to for her boss.

She'd worried about her colleagues at the Colby Agency. She genuinely cared about others. Dakota had lost that. He hadn't cared about anybody in a long, long time.

Maybe he no longer knew how. He was seriously damaged.

He mentally shook it off. Didn't matter. If he got her out of here alive that would be good enough.

He wasn't a hero.

Not the way she was.

He inhaled the fruity smell of her hair. She was something. He smiled in spite of himself. Maybe Lucky Malone hadn't ever been very lucky but she more than made up for it in determination and bravery.

Maybe they were more alike than he first thought.

Chapter Seventeen

3:48 a.m.

Lucas had questioned Maggie James until she'd broken down in tears. He'd known he was getting soft when guilt had driven him not only to comfort her but to apologize. She was an innocent in this catastrophe.

He'd pushed her too far. For nothing. Keaton had left her place around 2:00 a.m. How he'd gotten away without Jim or Lucas catching him was another indication that Lucas was not at the top of his game these days. Retirement had made him soft and slow. Jim had been distracted with updates from Simon and Ian.

He and Jim had driven back to the brownstone that served as the Equalizers headquarters and gone inside. Keaton hadn't bothered to have the locks changed. Jim still carried a key. Technically it was still breaking and entering but they didn't care.

"He's cautious," Jim commented when a second

search of Keaton's office turned up nothing in the way of personal information.

"And smart," Lucas admitted though it galled him to say so. "Whatever he's up to, he's gone to great lengths to cover his tracks."

Uncertainty haunted Lucas once more. What if he were wasting time? Victoria and Lucky were out there. There still had been no ransom demand or contact whatsoever from the bastard responsible for their disappearance. So far the Colby Agency had found nothing. *Nothing.*

Not once in thirty tears with the military and then the CIA had Lucas ever hit a brick wall like this.

"I know what you're thinking, Lucas."

He turned to his stepson. Jim had leaned against Keaton's desk. "We have nothing," he said, his voice tight with an unfamiliar emotion. Fear.

Lucas shook his head. "We have to be missing something."

"When a perp plans and then executes a move," Jim went on, his own voice weighted with worry, "typically there's a demand or contact of some sort. At the very least there's chatter out there. But this guy—" he glanced around the office that had once been his "—if it is this guy, has kept his plans to himself. No bragging. No coordinating the strategy. Nothing. It's impossible to track down clues when none are left behind."

As correct as Jim's assessment might be, it didn't

change the fact that they had nothing. More than eighteen hours missing and they had not one lead.

Lucas was about to say as much when his cell vibrated. Adrenaline shot through his veins. His gaze met Jim's expectant one as he answered.

"Byrd Institute," Ian Michaels, a second in command at the Colby Agency, announced. "We tracked down the ambulance driver who was called to transport a patient to the institute from the clinic where Victoria disappeared."

Lucas passed this info on to Jim. Then to Ian he said, "The driver wasn't aware the clinic was closed for renovations?"

"He was not. He assumed the call was legit."

The pause that followed trapped like a rock in Lucas's craw. "Did he identify the patient as Victoria?"

"Yes."

"Jim and I are on our way. I'll download the route on my phone." Lucas wasn't wasting another second. There were many questions to which he wanted answers but those would have to wait.

"Simon and I are already en route." He provided the address and quickest route from Lucas's location.

Lucas motioned to Jim. "We're right behind you."

"There's one other thing."

Lucas stopped cold at the grave sound of Ian's voice.

"Miss Malone was not with Victoria."

Dear God. That could mean only one thing.

Like the agency's driver and the others at that gruesome scene, Lucky was dead.

THE TRUCK STOPPED ABRUPTLY.

Victoria winced. Despite the cramped quarters she'd bumped her head. She wished she could move. Her entire body ached.

The driver's door slammed shut. Tension trembled through her as the truck shifted. The driver was climbing into the bed of the truck. She assumed it was the driver. Would it be Lucas or Jim? Anticipation lit in her belly. Thank God they had found her. And Lucky. Victoria smiled. She had gone above and beyond the call of duty. Thank God she hadn't been hurt. Wait. Victoria fought to clear her groggy mind. The drug they'd given her wasn't wearing off nearly quickly enough.

Lucky had gone back in. They could waste no time returning to that awful place to save her. And her friend Garrett. Who was this Garrett? How had Lucky come upon his help?

The door to the hidden compartment opened. Victoria blinked rapidly in an attempt to force her eyes to adjust and make out what she saw. A dim glow backlit the man leaning over her. Recognition nagged at her. He looked vaguely familiar, but she couldn't see him that well.

"Victoria, we have to move quickly." He reached out his hand to assist her.

"Who are you?"

"Once you're out of danger, I'll explain all you need to know."

Part of her wanted to hesitate. Who was this man? But she was no fool. She accepted his hand and allowed him to help her out of the constricted hiding place.

They were in a room...no, a garage. Small, nothing like the massive one Lucky had led her to. "Where are we?"

He kept her balanced as she stepped down to the concrete floor. She quickly checked her hospital gown to ensure it was fully closed.

"This way."

He guided her outside, then closed the garage door. The garage was connected to a small yellow ranch-style house. Another vehicle, a dark SUV, sat to the side of the gravel drive. When he hit the remote, the SUV's interior lights flashed as the doors unlocked. He opened the passenger-side door and assisted her into the seat.

As Victoria fastened her seat belt, she watched him climb behind the wheel and start the engine. She studied what she could see of his face until the interior light faded to darkness.

"Keaton." That was where she'd seen him. With Maggie James at the restaurant that night.

At the sound of his name he turned to her. The faint glow from the dash lights provided little insight as to what was on his mind.

"That's right." He flashed a brief smile. "Slade Keaton. I took over the Equalizers from your son."

Victoria recalled that Jim had said something to that effect. "Can you tell me what's going on now?"

He backed up the SUV, then rolled forward in the direction of the street. "Let's put some distance between us and the institute first." He braked at the end of the driveway.

"We have to go back."

Keaton slid something from his pocket and offered it to her. A cell phone. She stared at it in confusion.

"Call your family and let them know you're safe." His gaze locked with hers. "I'll take you home."

The urge to do just that was very nearly overwhelming. She accepted the phone but shook her head. "We have to go back for Lucky, my associate. She's still inside that place." Victoria shivered. Besides her ordeal, there was something evil about that so-called institute.

"That won't be necessary," Keaton assured. "I've prepared an egress for Miss Malone and my colleague, Dakota Garrett."

"Are you certain it will work?" Victoria wasn't going anywhere until she was absolutely certain.

Keaton powered down his window. "Listen for yourself."

She strained to hear but heard nothing save for the usual night sounds of crickets and the distant hum of interstate traffic. "I don't—"

The solid boom echoed in the air. She started to ask what that meant, but another thundering boom cut off the thought. Two more explosions followed.

Keaton powered the window closed. He turned to Victoria. "You should make that call now. I'm sure your family's worried."

Who was this man? Victoria pushed aside her questions and swiftly entered Lucas's cell number. The sound of his voice was all the guarantee Victoria needed. Whatever had happened these past twenty hours, Lucas would make it right.

She closed the phone. "Lucas is almost here. He would like us to wait at the upcoming intersection if it's safe to do so."

Keaton checked the rearview mirror. "I don't see a problem. We don't have a tail."

Victoria turned and stared out the rear window. She hadn't even thought to look. The drug was hindering her reactions.

Keaton drove to the intersection and parked on the side of the road facing the direction from which Lucas and Jim would arrive.

She relaxed for the first time in nearly twenty hours. Lucas would be here soon and he would get to the bottom of this unholy mess.

It was almost over.

Chapter Eighteen

"That's our cue."

Before Lucky could ask Garrett what he meant, he scrambled out of the laundry bin.

There had been four explosions somewhere on the grounds of the institute. Were they in a new kind of danger? Was this building next? Alarms were wailing.

"Hurry!"

Lucky took the hand he offered and climbed out. "What just happened?"

Garrett grinned. "He said he'd get me out." Garrett strode toward the tunnel with Lucky in tow. "But I didn't trust him to follow through."

Relief chased away the worry. Lucky grinned herself. "The Colby Agency always stands by its word." If Mr. Camp said he'd get them out, he would. No question.

Inside the massive garage, Garrett moved from one vehicle to the next and then appeared to search the room. It was so dark in there she didn't know how he expected to see what he was looking for. Keys, she figured.

He swore. "I guess the only way out is on foot. The vehicle keys are in lockup."

"Can we make it on foot?"

Garrett grabbed her hand again and hurried to the door she recalled that led to the outside. He cracked open the door just far enough for them to see. Two large buses had been moved to the side entrance of the institute's main building. He turned up the volume on the walkie-talkie and listened a moment to the frantic exchange.

"They're preparing to evacuate the patients if necessary." He turned to Lucky. "Don't go for the main gate. Security will be all over that. Look for any other avenue. Keaton probably blasted two or more holes in the wall."

"You can lead the way." She tightened her hold on his hand. No way was she going without him.

"You have to get out of here now." He shook off her hold. "I'll be right behind you, but first I have to finish some old business with Byrd."

He was serious. "The police will deal with Byrd." She grabbed his arm. "You can't go back in there."

"I have to make sure he's stopped. I saved myself once, this time I'm saving the others."

Lucky took a deep breath. "Fine. I'll help you." She thought about the colonel. Garrett was right. The patients had to be saved. Byrd had to be stopped now. The law could take weeks or months to stop him.

"No."

A frown worried her brow. "Why are we arguing? We're wasting time." He couldn't be serious.

"I want you out of here. Now."

Lucky folded her arms over her chest. "No way."

Garrett didn't argue for a moment. Lucky was pretty sure she'd won this one.

"I lied to you."

That frown marred deeper. "What?"

"I've been lying to you the whole time."

She shook her head. "What're you talking about?"

"Lucas Camp didn't send me. The Colby Agency had nothing to do with any of this. I was following you." He turned and stared out that narrow gap in the door. "When you and your driver were attacked I stepped in."

Lucky understood most of that. Why was he talking about this now? "You saved my life." That was exactly why she wasn't going to leave him to finish this alone.

"You don't get it. I didn't come here because I was trying to help you. I was following orders from my boss to rescue your boss. I told you Lucas had sent me to keep you appeased and to give you a reason not to contact your agency."

Her heart sank. This whole thing had been one big lie. "Who is your boss?"

"His name is Keaton. He runs a P.I. firm called the Equalizers. I'm one of his men."

She'd heard about the Equalizers. "Jim Colby's old firm."

Garrett nodded.

Lucky's breath trapped in her lungs. "What about Mrs. Colby-Camp? Was she taken to safety?"

"Keaton was determined to ensure her safety at all cost."

"So he would have contacted her family once he got her out of here."

Shouting outside drew his attention there. "What else would he do? Now go." He shifted his attention back to her. "You don't owe me anything."

The reality of his words sank in a little deeper, joining her heart in the proximity of her feet. All that time at the house he'd been lying. Anger churned inside her. "Were you ever really a patient here?" He'd insisted that going in alone was the only option. His history here had made him an expert. Any outside interference beyond his surgical attempt to rescue Mrs. Colby-Camp would almost certainly have resulted in a bad ending.

"Everything else I told you was the truth. Now go." He started back to the tunnel.

He'd lied to her. Lucky scrubbed her hands over her face. Dear God what would the folks at the agency think? All these hours that she and her boss had been missing and they hadn't had a clue where they were or if they were even alive. Lucky should have made that call.

She wanted to run after Garrett and punch him

out. Fury tightened her fingers into fists. She wanted
to kick his boss's butt. Who the heck did Keaton
think he was?

Taking a breath, she relaxed her tense muscles.
Unfortunately right now there was something far
more important she had to do.

Lucky rushed after Garrett, taking the stairs two
at a time. She raced along the tunnel until she could
see Garrett nearing the far end. He stopped, turned
around and stared at her.

She didn't slow down until she stood directly in
front of him. He looked annoyed. Good, because
she was, too. Without preamble, she reached out and
slapped his face.

He flinched.

"That was for lying to me." She smoothed her
stinging hand over her hair and managed to compose
herself somewhat. "Now, let's go get this done."

Maybe it was confusion, maybe it was disbelief,
but he stared at her with the strangest expression on
his face. "Are you insane?"

What kind of question was that? She straightened
her scrub top and her badge. "I'm the one who has
the badge and the uniform. I can provide cover. What
have you got?" Let him top that.

His gaze narrowed as he searched hers for two
then three beats. He reached behind him and pulled
a weapon from his waistband. "I've got the gun."

"Great. That should cover all the bases, then. Now,

let's do this thing." She walked around him and toward the door.

He didn't try to stop her. A few steps later she felt him following her. Confusion whirled in her head, along with a dozen other emotions. She wasn't sure how to feel. She had absolutely no reason to trust Garrett. He'd lied to her repeatedly. At the moment none of that mattered. Stopping evil was the only goal that counted.

And, whatever his motive, Garrett had saved her life and Victoria's. She owed him.

THE EMERGENCY LIGHTS had kicked in. The alarm buzzed loudly and distinctly enough to alert the staff without panicking the patients. The corridor on the lower level remained clear. Evacuation protocol dictated that floors one through four were vacated first. Research was dead last.

Literally.

Dakota knew Byrd would terminate those patients before he would risk exposing his secret work to the authorities.

At the double doors Dakota swiped the badge he lifted from the goon Byrd had left in charge of securing him. The entry marked Authorized Personnel Only opened. He gestured for Malone to stay behind him as he moved forward. With the weapon palmed he weaved from door to door to check the patients who lay beyond. One swipe at each door and he had access.

Most were heavily sedated and well secured to their beds. The silenced monitoring equipment showed patterns of vitals. Dakota resisted the impulse to hold his breath. The smell of death hung in every room.

Ten patients. The last two treatment rooms were vacant.

Dakota headed for his ultimate destination. Byrd's secret office—the place where he kept his research files. The evidence of his dirty work.

Two yards from Byrd's office Dakota stilled. The door was partially open. He checked the other end of the corridor. Still deserted. This didn't feel right.

Malone moved up close behind him. He pressed a finger to his lips, then he listened. A soft whir filtered past the open door. Dakota mentally sifted through the possibilities. Then he recognized the sound.

He pointed to his eyes and then the corridor with his free hand to put Malone on lookout. Adopting a fire-ready posture he charged through the door. He leveled his aim on the back of the man who was busily feeding the paper shredder. "Hands up."

The man froze but didn't comply. He was too tall to be Byrd. Probably one of his trusted goons.

"Do it now," Dakota ordered.

The man dropped the pages and raised his hands in the universal gesture of surrender. Dakota eased close enough to check him for a weapon. He lifted the handgun from its holster and tucked it into his waistband. The walkie-talkie was next. Dakota turned it off and tossed it across the room.

"Where's your boss?"

"Go to hell."

He was going to play it that way, was he? Dakota rammed the muzzle into the back of his skull. "Where is Byrd?"

"You heard me."

Loyalty. Even among criminals.

"Have it your way." Dakota wrapped an arm around his neck and rendered him unconscious. Once he was down he dragged him behind the desk and secured him. Many things could be accomplished with a leather belt, including binding hands and feet behind one's back. A necktie made a handy gag.

Malone barged in. "Someone's coming."

Satisfied with his handiwork, Dakota stood. "How many?"

"I don't know. I ducked in here as soon as I saw the double doors opening. I was afraid they would see me."

"Good thinking." He glanced around the room. There was no place for her to hide. He nodded to the open door. "Hide behind the door." As she obeyed he moved toward her. He passed her the gun he'd lifted from the guy behind the desk. "I took it off safety. No matter what you hear, don't come out. If things don't go well, wait until it's clear and get out of here."

He started to ease the door closer to the wall, ensuring she wouldn't be seen. She stopped him. "You do that every time." She searched his eyes. "For a liar and a guy who cares about nothing but accomplishing the mission, you sure seem to like playing the hero."

What the hell? "You are nuts, do you know that?" Quick steps echoed in the corridor.

"I'm just saying."

What was it about this woman? In the next second he realized he was the one who was crazy. He grabbed her by the chin and kissed her hard and fast. He'd done this once already. Once made him crazy; twice made him stupid. "Now stay quiet." While she stared, dazed, at him, he eased the door back enough to tightly sandwich her between it and the wall.

Since he didn't have a better plan, he took a seat behind Byrd's fancy desk. He took a bead on the open doorway. Dakota wasn't opposed to taking out whoever entered.

Byrd, followed by two of his muscled-up associates, stormed into the room. The surprise on Byrd's face was worth whatever happened next. Dakota centered his bead right between the madman's eyes.

The threesome stalled just inside the door. Weapons were drawn.

"You escaped," Byrd snarled.

Dakota shrugged. "I came back. I missed you."

Byrd smirked. "You're a dead man, Eaton. You crossed the wrong person this time. Mr. Murray was quite generous to the institute for such a brief use of our facilities. He was most displeased when you fled with the prized addition to his collection. He had been waiting a very long time to include his old enemy Lucas Camp to his trophy case. His wife was the key to success and you took that from him. He and his men are searching the surrounding area for you even as we speak."

"Too late. Victoria Colby-Camp is way out of his reach now."

Byrd dared to step toward him. His backup took that same step deeper into the room. "You must have had a partner. Someone on my staff. I will know the name."

Dakota hitched a thumb toward the papers scattered on the floor. "I'd say you have bigger problems. You know the police will arrive soon. No way those explosions will be ignored."

"They're en route now," Byrd returned. "I called them myself. When they arrive they will find the body of a disgruntled former patient who tried to blow up the institute."

"We'll die together," Dakota suggested. "Give them something to sink their investigative teeth into."

"Shoot him," Byrd ordered.

The door slammed shut.

A shot exploded. The man to the left of Byrd stumbled back as he spun around, catching the bullet in the shoulder. The one on the right started to fire. Dakota dropped him even as two more shots blasted from the weapon Malone wielded. A bullet plowed into the desktop. Dakota scrambled back. Damn that was close.

"Get down on the floor," Malone shouted.

The wounded man dropped his weapon and took a facedown position on the floor.

"Get up," Byrd screamed to no avail at his injured guard.

Dakota came around the desk, his weapon trained on the bastard who liked playing God. "On the floor," he ordered. When Byrd didn't comply, Dakota took great satisfaction in knocking his lights out. He was on the floor then.

"Check him." Dakota nodded to the man Lucky had wounded. "Make sure he has no other weapons. And check his pockets for anything we can use to secure the three of them." Dakota checked the guard he'd put down. Still alive. The gash on his forehead explained his state of unconsciousness. He must have hit his head on the way down.

"Will these work?"

Malone had found a couple pairs of nylon hand-cuffs. "That'll work." Dakota secured both guards. He dug two more pair of the cuffs from the second guard's pockets. He secured Byrd and then, just to be safe, added a pair to the guard under the desk.

The chatter on the walkie-talkie snagged his attention. The police were on-site.

Dakota ushered Malone into the corridor. He visually checked the double doors to make sure no one was coming yet. "You stay here," he said to Malone. "Explain everything to the police. I have to go."

She shook her head. "Why? You're the one who saved the day. You should be here."

"There are things in my past that could muddy the waters and create some major waves that I don't need." He shrugged. "You don't need me for this."

"Does it have something to do with the name Eaton?"

"Yeah."

"I understand. You're not that person anymore." She smiled. "I know who you are. You're a hero."

He shook his head even as a smile tugged at his lips. "You're the hero."

She waved him off. "Go. I'll be fine."

He stepped back before he did something else stupid like kiss her a third time. "A pleasure working with you, Malone."

He walked away.

This mission was done. There was no reason for him to stay.

Before those double doors closed behind him he looked back. Malone was watching him go.

For the first time in his adult life Dakota suffered a twinge of doubt.

The doors closed, blocking his view of Malone.

It was done.

There was no going back.

Chapter Nineteen

The Colby Agency
Friday, June 3rd,

5:22 p.m.

Victoria studied the two men seated across the conference table. Slade Keaton had agreed to meet with her, Lucas and Jim to explain how he happened upon her abduction. Simon and Ian had wanted to sit in but that would have prompted an air of distrust and unfair odds. She wanted this meeting to be relaxed and open.

Dakota Garrett sat next to Keaton. Lucas and Jim were seated on either side of Victoria.

"This was quite a complicated event to explain to the Chicago P.D.," Victoria reminded. "They are not pleased with the length of time they were left in the dark."

Keaton nodded. "I appreciate your assistance in smoothing over that situation. We did what we had to do. My representative took no pleasure in any of the deceit or violence required to produce this outcome."

Victoria glanced at Garrett. He had explained each step he'd taken. That he had saved Lucky's life meant a great deal to Victoria.

"I'm still a little unclear about how you became aware of Murray's plans."

Victoria looked at her husband when he spoke. She knew Lucas did not trust Keaton in the least. He had been convinced that Keaton himself was responsible for Victoria's abduction. His stiff posture as well as the fury simmering in his tone even now made his position all too clear.

Keaton smiled. "I have numerous contacts. This is not the first time Murray and I have crossed paths. I needed to be sure what he was up to. My intel was sketchy at best. What I knew for certain was that Murray was plotting against the Colby Agency. Nothing beyond that. I had no choice but to look into the situation. As Maggie told you, I've been watching for some time, but I had nothing substantial to convey to you. If my intel turned out to be nothing, I had lost nothing. Sitting in Maggie's coffee shop keeping watch was no hardship."

When Lucas questioned Maggie James, she had told him as much. If Keaton were lying, he had gone to great lengths to cover his true motive.

Keaton continued. "Once the first domino fell, there was no time to do anything but follow through. Considering the unpredictable nature of the situation,

I felt compelled to handle it as a shadow operation. Your involvement," he said to Lucas, "or that of the police may have triggered tragedy. As you well know, Murray has a reputation for hair-trigger decisions that end badly."

"It seems rather convenient that Murray and his associates were captured only a few miles away by Homeland Security agents," Jim countered.

Victoria's son was not so ready to accept Keaton's story, either. Particularly the part about not bringing in the Colby Agency due to the precarious nature of the involvement of the Byrd Institute. According to Lucas, Murray's MO was to use facilities available locally to accomplish his evil work. Throwing around money gave him that feeling of power to which he was addicted.

"He had lost. Once the police arrived he had no reason to risk capture so he fled. I took the liberty of having one of my contacts from Homeland Security standing by. I was aware that HS had long wanted to get their hands on Murray."

"Yet," Jim countered once more, "you didn't feel comfortable contacting us."

Keaton smiled. "I have many contacts whom I know extremely well and with whom I have worked many times. With all due respect," he dipped his head, "I don't know you that well."

The answer didn't sit well with Jim but he didn't argue further.

"I'm curious," Lucas said. "How did you come to

have the sort of contacts who would know men like Murray?"

Murray was one of Lucas's oldest enemies. They'd once worked together in the CIA. Lucas had moved up the ranks while Murray's career had stalled. Once he'd crossed the line and joined the enemy, he'd blamed Lucas for his every failed operation. That was Victoria's biggest worry. Lucas had spent a lifetime serving his country and making evil enemies. Now he was retired and those still inside the government weren't at liberty to disclose intelligence. Like the people who had taken Murray into custody. Lucas had hit a brick wall in his attempt to get answers. The intelligence world was a different place these days.

Keaton smiled again, the expression at once charming and cocky. "I'm afraid the answer to that question is classified. I'm sure you understand."

"Well." Victoria stood. The men immediately followed suit. "Thank you for clearing up matters. This agency owes you a great deal, sir." She extended her hand.

Keaton shook her hand, his grasp firm and confident. "Not at all, Victoria. I only did what was right."

"As you say, we don't know each other very well. We need to change that." Victoria turned to Dakota then. "There are no words that accurately articulate my gratitude, Mr. Garrett."

"No problem, ma'am." He shook Victoria's hand.

Jim and Lucas exchanged handshakes with Keaton and Garrett.

"I hope we'll work together again in the future," Keaton ventured.

"Next time we'll be sure the lines of communication are kept open," Lucas warned.

"Of course," Keaton agreed.

As Jim escorted their guests to the lobby, Lucas turned to Victoria. "I don't trust him. My contact was certain that something about him was of interest to me."

Victoria couldn't argue with his reasoning. It saddened her that their driver and Lucas's old friend had lost their lives in this tragedy. That, too, was Murray's MO—never leave loose ends. "Time will provide the insight we need."

Lucas nodded, his expression grave. Then he smiled. "Whoever this guy is, I'm just glad you're safe."

Victoria stepped into his open arms. "That makes two of us." She was so thankful to be home.

Lucas drew back. He lifted her chin to look into her eyes. "I hope you won't ever try to protect me again when it comes to your health."

She shook her head. "I learned my lesson. You don't have to worry about that." Victoria was as healthy as a horse. Those horrifying test results that had indicated the possibility of cancer had been tampered with. Considering all that had happened, Dr. Klein had checked with the lab just to be certain. The lab had sent results indicating no cancer. Apparently the tampering had occurred between leaving the lab and arriving at the doctor's office.

Lucas kissed her lips. "Perhaps Keaton is all he says he is."

"Perhaps," Victoria agreed.

But she would be watching Mr. Keaton. As she knew Lucas would. Very closely.

Chapter Twenty

6:45 p.m.

Lucky hauled her bowl of popcorn to her sofa and curled up in preparation for mind-numbing hours of television. She was still exhausted.

The agency had given her an extra-long weekend. She didn't have to return to work until Wednesday. She raised a handful of popcorn to her lips. Instantly her mind swept her away from the reality show on the screen to when Garrett had kissed her. She shivered.

She hadn't seen him since he'd disappeared through those white double doors. Lucky had gone over every single detail of their time together. She'd repeated the details of their adventure, if you will, twice to the powers that be at the agency and to the police. Her bosses had assured her that she'd done the only thing she could. Both Mr. Camp and Mrs. Colby-Camp, as well as her son, had praised Lucky for her part in the operation.

She had passed Lucas's contact's message to him.

The statement *Tell Lucas I can't help him* seemed to disturb him greatly. He'd apologized for putting Lucky in that position. The way she saw it, his sending her had ultimately helped with the rescue.

And she'd met Garrett.

Not that anything would ever come of it, but he'd awakened feelings in her that she hadn't expected to ever feel. Truth was, she kind of missed him.

The doorbell buzzed, dragging her from those warm thoughts. Someone from the agency was likely checking on her again. They'd been doing that all afternoon. She set her popcorn aside and walked to the door. Her apartment was a wreck. She'd clean it later. She deserved this break.

She checked the security peephole and barely suppressed a squeal. It was Garrett. She took a breath, calmed herself, then opened the door.

"Garrett, what's up?" She was trying hard for nonchalance.

"Is it okay if I come in?"

She almost laughed. Usually he told her what he was going to do. "Sure." She opened the door wider, then closed it behind him.

He surveyed her living room and the adjoining kitchen. "Cute."

Cute? "Thanks." She supposed. "It's kind of small but it's all I need."

He nodded.

Where was her head? "Have a seat." She gestured to the bowl on the coffee table. "Would you like some popcorn?" She didn't have any beer or wine. "Iced tea?"

He shook his head. "No, thanks."

He wasn't going to sit down. Disappointment dragged at her chest. Why was he here? Clearly not for the reason she'd hoped.

"I came by to see how you're doing."

Her hopes wilted completely. "Oh. I'm fine. You?" How lame was that?

"I'm good. I quit my job."

But he'd been so good at it. "Really? Why?" How nosy was that? Maybe he didn't want to talk about it.

He shook his head. "Too much deception. My boss and I don't see eye-to-eye on things." A sigh whispered past his lips. "Mainly, I just don't want that life anymore. There are other opportunities out there."

Fear claimed her. Did that mean he was leaving Chicago. "Are you leaving Chicago?" She could have died at how desperate she sounded.

"No." A tiny smile cracked his lips. "Whatever I do, I'll do it here."

Relief. "That's great."

Silence.

"My boss," she began in an attempt to break the awkwardness, "says the FBI is all over Byrd and his institute. All the patients are being transferred and their families contacted."

"Yeah, I got that update."

What did she say now?

"So you're good with how things turned out?"

"Sure." He shoved his hands into his pockets. "Look, I wondered if you'd like to have dinner." He shrugged. "Or catch a movie."

Hope resurrected, making her breath catch. "Yeah. Either one."

"Good. Where would you like to go for dinner?"

She had to change. Her cheeks heated at the idea that she was wearing ragged jeans, her favorite lay-around-the-house pair, and an ancient T-shirt.

"You pick." She backed up a step. "I should change."

"Before you rush off…" He captured her arm and pulled her back the step she'd taken and then another, until their bodies were almost touching. "I just wanted to say that I really like you, Malone. I'd like to spend a lot more time with you."

"Lucky," she said, trying her best not to wring her hands. "You should call me Lucky."

He nodded. "Dakota Garrett. You can call me either one."

A smile tugged at her lips. "I like you, too." She licked her lips, tried to moisten her throat. Her heart was pounding so hard. "I'm really glad we're going to dinner."

The smile that stretched across his lips caused that little flutter in her chest. "That's good to hear."

"Okay." She hitched a thumb behind her. "I'll go change and we'll be on our way."

He held on to her hand when she would have pulled away. "One more thing."

She looked at him expectantly and found herself holding her breath.

"Before we go I'd like to fast-forward for maybe five minutes."

"Fast-forward?"

"To the end of the night where I walk you to your door and say good-night."

"Okay." She'd dreamed of kissing him again.

He pulled her into his arms, leaned down and covered her lips with his own. This kiss was nothing like the others. He took his time. And she sank against him for more of his taste. She'd never known a man like Dakota Garrett. Lucky couldn't wait to see where this new adventure took them. She draped her arms around his neck, and his arms tightened around her.

For the first time Lucky wasn't afraid to take the risk. Garrett had already proven that he would never let her down. He was the real thing—a true hero.

* * * * *

INTRIGUE

COMING NEXT MONTH

Available June 14, 2011

#1281 COWBOY BRIGADE
Daddy Corps
Elle James

#1282 LASSOED
Whitehorse, Montana: Chisholm Cattle Company
B.J. Daniels

#1283 BROKEN
Colby Agency: The New Equalizers
Debra Webb

#1284 THE MISSING TWIN
Guardian Angel Investigations: Lost and Found
Rita Herron

#1285 COOPER VENGEANCE
Cooper Justice: Cold Case Investigation
Paula Graves

#1286 CAPTURING THE COMMANDO
Colleen Thompson

HICNM0511

REQUEST YOUR FREE BOOKS!
2 FREE NOVELS PLUS 2 FREE GIFTS!

♦ Harlequin®
INTRIGUE®

BREATHTAKING ROMANTIC SUSPENSE

YES! Please send me 2 FREE Harlequin Intrigue® novels and my 2 FREE gifts (gifts are worth about $10). After receiving them, if I don't wish to receive any more books, I can return the shipping statement marked "cancel." If I don't cancel, I will receive 6 brand-new novels every month and be billed just $4.24 per book in the U.S. or $4.99 per book in Canada. That's a saving of at least 15% off the cover price! It's quite a bargain! Shipping and handling is just 50¢ per book in the U.S. and 75¢ per book in Canada.* I understand that accepting the 2 free books and gifts places me under no obligation to buy anything. I can always return a shipment and cancel at any time. Even if I never buy another book, the two free books and gifts are mine to keep forever.

182/382 HDN FC5H

Name _____ (PLEASE PRINT)

Address _____ Apt. #

City _____ State/Prov. _____ Zip/Postal Code

Signature (if under 18, a parent or guardian must sign)

Mail to the **Reader Service:**
IN U.S.A.: P.O. Box 1867, Buffalo, NY 14240-1867
IN CANADA: P.O. Box 609, Fort Erie, Ontario L2A 5X3

Not valid for current subscribers to Harlequin Intrigue books.

**Are you a subscriber to Harlequin Intrigue books
and want to receive the larger-print edition?
Call 1-800-873-8635 or visit www.ReaderService.com.**

* Terms and prices subject to change without notice. Prices do not include applicable taxes. Sales tax applicable in N.Y. Canadian residents will be charged applicable taxes. Offer not valid in Quebec. This offer is limited to one order per household. All orders subject to credit approval. Credit or debit balances in a customer's account(s) may be offset by any other outstanding balance owed by or to the customer. Please allow 4 to 6 weeks for delivery. Offer available while quantities last.

Your Privacy—The Reader Service is committed to protecting your privacy. Our Privacy Policy is available online at www.ReaderService.com or upon request from the Reader Service.

We make a portion of our mailing list available to reputable third parties that offer products we believe may interest you. If you prefer that we not exchange your name with third parties, or if you wish to clarify or modify your communication preferences, please visit us at www.ReaderService.com/consumerschoice or write to us at Reader Service Preference Service, P.O. Box 9062, Buffalo, NY 14269. Include your complete name and address.

HII1

Harlequin® Blaze™ brings you
New York Times *and* USA TODAY *bestselling author*
Vicki Lewis Thompson with three new steamy titles
from the bestselling miniseries SONS OF CHANCE

Chance isn't just the last name of these rugged
Wyoming cowboys—it's their motto, too!

Read on for a sneak peek at the first title,
SHOULD'VE BEEN A COWBOY

Available June 2011 only from Harlequin® Blaze™.

"THANKS FOR NOT TURNING ON THE LIGHTS," Tyler said. "I'm a mess."

"Not in my book." Even in low light, Alex had a good view of her yellow shirt plastered to her body. It was all he could do not to reach for her, mud and all. But the next move needed to be hers, not his.

She slicked her wet hair back and squeezed some water out of the ends as she glanced upward. "I like the sound of the rain on a tin roof."

"Me, too."

She met his gaze briefly and looked away. "Where's the sink?"

"At the far end, beyond the last stall."

Tyler's running shoes squished as she walked down the aisle between the rows of stalls. She glanced sideways at Alex. "So how much of a cowboy are you these days? Do you ride the range and stuff?"

"I ride." He liked being able to say that. "Why?"

"Just wondered. Last summer, you were still a city boy. You even told me you weren't the cowboy type, but you're…different now."

He wasn't sure if that was a good thing or a bad thing. Maybe she preferred city boys to cowboys. "How am I different?"

"Well, you dress differently, and your hair's a little longer. Your face seems a little more chiseled, but maybe that's because of your hair. Also, there's something else, something harder to define, an attitude…"

"Are you saying I have an attitude?"

"Not in a bad way. It's more like a quiet confidence."

He was flattered, but still he had to laugh. "I just admitted a while ago that I have all kinds of doubts about this event tomorrow. That doesn't seem like quiet confidence to me."

"This isn't about your job, it's about…your…" She took a deep breath. "It's about your sex appeal, okay? I have no business talking about it, because it will only make me want to do things I shouldn't do." She started toward the end of the barn. "Now, where's that sink? We need to get cleaned up and go back to the house. Dinner is probably ready, and I—"

He spun her around and pulled her into his arms, mud and all. "Let's do those things." Then he kissed her, knowing that she would kiss him back, knowing that this time he would take that kiss where he wanted it to go. And she would let him.

Follow Tyler and Alex's wild adventures in
SHOULD'VE BEEN A COWBOY
Available June 2011 only from Harlequin® Blaze™
wherever books are sold.

INTRIGUE

SPECIAL EDITION

Life, Love and Family

LOVE CAN BE FOUND IN THE MOST UNLIKELY PLACES, ESPECIALLY WHEN YOU'RE NOT LOOKING FOR IT...

Failed marriages, broken families and disappointment. Cecilia and Brandon have both been unlucky in love and life and are ripe for an intervention. Good thing Brandon's mother happens to stumble upon this matchmaking project. But will Brandon be able to open his eyes and get away from his busy career to see that all he needs is right there in front of him?

FIND OUT IN

WHAT THE SINGLE DAD WANTS...

BY *USA TODAY* BESTSELLING AUTHOR

MARIE FERRARELLA

AVAILABLE IN JUNE 2011
WHEREVER BOOKS ARE SOLD.